Enjoy!
John P. Schulz

REQUIEM FOR A REDNECK

REQUIEM
for a REDNECK

A Novel by

JOHN P. SCHULZ

WHEREDEPONY PRESS
Rome, GA

ACKNOWLEDGEMENTS

I would like to thank my wonderful editor and companion, Dekie Hicks, for her tireless efforts to make my writing look its best, my son, John Robert Schulz for his thoughtful artwork and page design, and my other son, Paul Schulz, for sharing elements of his well-honed sense of humor. My brother, Tom Schulz, helped by allowing me to listen to him telling my mother how to go about producing and marketing a book. Thanks, Tom. Thank you to my sister, Mary deWit, for all of her help and support. I would like to extend a special thanks to my research assistant, Eugene "Bud" Sims, who introduced me to some of the devious thought processes of the Georgia Redneck, and Tommy Cobb, who contributed to the story by helping me figure out how to get a leg removed. Thanks to Bob and Micheline Hicks, Nelson and Yolanda Magee, Sam and Virginia Spector, Ginger Grant, and others who read installments and encouraged me in my efforts. Thanks to John Carter who once said, "Your life is a book, John, write it."

John P. Schulz | June, 2008

WHEREDEPONY PRESS
P.O. Box 1194, Rome GA 30162 USA
www.wheredeponypress.com

ISBN 978-0-9818252-0-5
Library of Congress Control Number: 2001012345

Edited by Dekie Hicks
Cover and chapter illustrations, graphic design by John Robert Schulz

To my mother, Dr. Jane B. Schulz

She told me stories
She read me stories
And then she set me free,
to live a story of my own

CONTENTS

chapter **1**

HARCE 2003

When they found his leg in the poison ivy patch, they knew they were close. One of the cops hollered out, "Hey, John, what does Harce's leg look like?"

I started in his direction, answering, "Blue titanium with a rounded plate on the bottom. Kind of like it was made out of the shank from an expensive tennis racket."

"Well, come over here and look."

I looked at the undergrowth in the clearing where the cop was standing.

"No, you come over here," I yelled. "Didn't your daddy teach you about poison ivy?"

The cop jumped back and ran out to where I stood. He must have been a Yankee. He was holding the leg. It looked like Harce's leg, but there was one way to make sure.

I pointed. "Turn it over and look just above where the ankle would be. There should be a small, almost invisible sliding plate. That's where he kept his pot."

A detective walked up and examined the leg. He found the plate and slid it to the side, obviously admiring the craftsmanship. The hole was empty.

Bud had called me that morning and told me that the police

needed help finding Harce. They had found his truck stuck in a ditch and figured he was lost in the woods behind the bauxite quarries. Bud and I knew he wasn't lost. We knew something bad was wrong. Harce would never get lost in those woods.

Bud explained it to the detective, "Officer, there ain't no way Harce got lost in them woods. He was a carpenter—"

"Bud, what does that have to do with it?"

"I'm getting there, officer. You see, Harce could build anything you want. Do a real good job, too. But he never understood fences."

"Bud, I don't see how that enters into—"

Bud bowed up. His face turned red, and he got that look on his face that told the detective to shut up. "Jest give me a damn minute and I'll tell you. You see, Harce couldn't never build a fence that was worth a damn and his cows and hogs and chickens kept getting out. Before his leg got cut off, he chased every animal he ever had all over every square inch of this mountain. He knew these woods. He knew them like the back of his hand. He knew these woods so well that you sumbitches never even found his dope patch or his still. He ain't lost."

They found Harce's body about an hour later. He had crawled up under some brush that had fallen across a ditch. They pried his cell phone from his stiff fingers. The detective checked to see who Harce had called last.

I looked at the number. I looked at the detective. "That's my number," I said. "He called me the night before last." I knew right then what had happened.

Bud looked at me and said, "Aw, hell, John. Does that mean—?"

And now you know that Harce is dead. Now I can tell you about him and not have to come up to the end of the story and say something like: "Oh, yeah, Harce died." Nobody likes that part.

But Harce was the one who started me writing again. I have a debt to pay.

Before I quit drinking, before I kicked him out, Harce used to come over to the house and sit by the wood heater, start on a six pack and say, "Hey, John, tell me a story."

chapter **2** THE COLONS 1993

Harce always liked a good story. We traded many of them back and forth over the ten years or so of our friendship. Now it is time to tell the story about Harce and his "old lady," Louann, and his friends.

1993 was when the big snow storm came in March. Pine and cedar trees fell all over the place. They were in the lake in the front yard, across the driveway, and all across Bell's Ferry Road for miles. All of the neighbors brought chain saws and pick up trucks to help each other clean up the mess. It took weeks.

As soon as we could get out of the driveway and after we had chain sawed and cleaned up 30 large cedar trees, we decided that we had to go see Jerry. I had always had an interest in woodworking and I just couldn't make myself throw the large cedar trunks on the fire, but I didn't know where to find a saw mill.

I knew Jerry would know where to find a saw mill. I didn't really want to go see Jerry. He was a bank robber who had been out of jail for a few years. He made his living loan sharking, selling cars, bootlegging Sunday beer, and pushing a few pills that were in high demand. Jerry wasn't so tall, but he was big with arms like tree trunks. He was tattooed and he had a long white beard with a diabolic brown tobacco stain that looked like a goatee in a field of snow. He did business from a rocking chair on his front porch in the halfway renovated mill village.

Jerry knew everybody.

Jerry leaned back in his rocking chair on the porch and grinned. "You got a gun, John?"

I told him I had no use for one.

He pulled out the biggest pistol I had ever seen. "If you goin' to The Colons, you might need this here hogleg."

I told Jerry to keep it. I wouldn't know what to do with it even if I did need it and I had always been able to get by with a big grin and the unstated bluff offered by my six foot four inch frame. I always take a nice plant when I go to meet someone new. Rednecks like plants.

"Well, you get on Hermitage Road, cross the 53 four lane, and head up into The Colons. You ever been to The Colons before? I didn't think so." Jerry gave me complete directions to find the sawmill.

He warned me, though, that the man's name was Harce and it must be pronounced in that manner. Jerry said that if I wanted a fight to call the guy "Horace" with an O and with two syllables. I didn't really want a fight. When I got there, I found out how much I really didn't want a fight.

We loaded about ten of the cedar logs in Marsha's red and black 1982 Ford F150. She calls it her "Bulldog truck" because she's the ultimate Georgia Bulldog fan. To this day, she doesn't want another truck.

The first thing of significance that happened on the trip was that Marsha gunned the truck going across the four lane and six of the logs fell out in a straight line, blocking traffic in both directions. We loaded the logs back on while these "type A" businessmen in a hurry honked and yelled. They didn't even try to help. Must have been a bunch of Yankees. We reloaded, I tripped and spilled my beer, and then we headed for The Colons.

Hermitage Road is like a river running through a valley. It meanders and at times I expected to see our own tail lights in the curve ahead. There was a straight-up drainage ditch on each side of the road which kept getting deeper and deeper as the road became narrower and narrower. To the right and the left, moss-covered hills dripping with moisture went up and up into a barrier of second growth oak and sweet gum trees with sporadic clusters of various types of ferns. Silver mounds of lichen that the old ladies call "reindeer moss" added texture and interest to the overall collage. At intervals to the right and left, I could see moss covered ruts where the logging trucks had removed everything that even looked like a pine tree maybe fifteen years before. The pines were obviously never replanted. I wanted to take a picture, but there had only been room in the truck for either the camera case or the beer cooler. The camera had stayed at the house.

Marsha closed her eyes and aimed the truck toward the center as we crossed the one lane bridge with no railing that Jerry had told us about and took the next left onto Firetower Road. We immediately started appreciating the narrow asphalt road that we had just turned off of. To quote Bud, "I was so uptight you couldn't of drove a needle up my ass with a sledge hammer." We had entered The Colons.

The road was made of chert and was obviously converted from paths followed by logging trucks. Chert is a wonderful road builder if it is maintained. An old man had once told me that chert was "rocks mixed with dirt that's waiting to be rocks." Part of a chert rock may look like a piece of flint embedded in dirty, white kiln-fired clay. I asked a geologist about chert one time and he used the term "cryptocrystalline quartz." In North Georgia, "chert" means a mixture of small gravel with a clay-like filling that is used for a driveway or a road base. When chert is spread and packed, it is similar to a good gravel bed. The entire mountainside in The Colons is chert. If you want to plant a tree or put in a fence post, the best tool will not be a post-hole digger or a shovel, it will be a digging bar. You raise the digging bar way up in the air and jam it straight down into the ground. Then you wiggle it around, loosening the stuff that is waiting to be rocks and prying up the stuff that has already become rock. A shovel is then used to remove the loose stuff.

It takes a special kind of plant to grow in the chert on the hillsides. Pine trees can handle it with their large tap roots and birds drop oak, sweet gum and cedar seeds in the blanket of pine straw so that over time a multitude of small, light-starved trees forms a thicket under the pines. Then, Georgia Kraft sends the pulpwooders to cut and haul the pine out for paper and cardboard. What they do is called "clear cutting" and when the loggers are finished it looks like a tornado has run through. There are pine tree tops and hardwood saplings that the machinery has pushed sideways. Over time, the hardwood trees and cedars straighten up and, with the new availability of light, form a hardwood forest. The leaves that drop each autumn help keep down the growth of honeysuckle and saw brier while also forming a layer of "duff" on top of the chert, which is a perfect environment for fern spores to germinate and thrive.

That's the picture of The Colons. The sides of the roads were formed from dirt pushed aside by the bulldozers making room for the logging trucks years ago. Nothing woody wants to grow on the sides of the road which means there is no competition for the myriad varieties of mosses and lichens which slowly form a green mat over the slope, nurtured by the water which constantly runs from the hill because it can't penetrate the dirt and which brings nitrogen from the rotting leaves of the hardwoods.

The chert road had not been maintained. It was wide enough, but that was necessary because a lot of room was needed for dodging the potholes and ruts. There were some holes that would eat a tandem dump truck for lunch, and sideways ruts that resembled a miniature version of the Grand Canyon. We had to stop periodically to adjust the load of cedar logs. I didn't want any of them to fall off in that place. Marsha drove as carefully as possible while I sat and figured out how much the front end repair work on the truck was going to cost. But we got there. Jerry's directions were right on the money.

"Right around the fifth left turn," he had said, "swing way to the right to keep from sliding down the rut into a ditch because there ain't no wrecker that'll go up there to get you out. You'll see a split rail fence."

If you had asked me before if I had ever seen a split rail fence, I would have replied, "Of course, I've seen a lot of split rail fences." But I would have been wrong. This was THE split rail fence. We stopped to examine it. It was made of cedar. The rails were obviously hand-hewn. The posts were carefully selected, sanded and polished. All of the parts were slotted and doweled and fit together so perfectly that a piece of paper wouldn't slide between them. All of the work appeared to have been done by non-motorized hand tools.

After studying the posts and rails, I looked up to see Marsha admiring the trained, pruned, and groomed Lady Banksia roses which filled in every third section of the fence. Somehow, this was not quite what we had expected. We soon learned expectations never bore fruit in The Colons.

chapter

3 THE SAWMILL

We pulled into the driveway which led to a rather large parking lot. Marsha parked next to a disreputable logging truck that had once been red, maybe. I reached for the door handle and then reconsidered immediately. I really never knew the difference between rottweilers and pit bulls, but two of them were suddenly guarding the truck doors, silently standing there with their teeth bared, waiting for the action that would obviously start the minute I set foot outside of the truck. We decided that it would be a good time to sit still and wait a bit. I found courage in a fresh can of beer and Marsha just sat there with a funny look on her face. I turned to look behind us and saw a third dog staring through the back window of the pickup. I took a swig of beer and decided to look around at the setting. There was a lot to look at.

Off to the right was what I might call a log cabin. It was two stories high with a large front porch. The logs were cut square with concrete chinking between the mitered joints. The beginning of a large gazebo stood in front of the porch. Off to the left of the house was a pergola covering the distance from the house to a magnificent barbecue pit. Some of the best smelling smoke in the world poured out of the brick chimney. Several wooden swings hung from the pergola with five or six men in flannel shirts, boots and well worn-jeans rocking, smoking, drinking beer, and staring at us. As I looked, a woman appeared in the doorway of the house, leaning against the door jamb, scowling. I found out later that Louann always checked any newcomers and that she always looked like she was scowling because she was sensitive about her teeth.

"Harce, call them dogs."

One of the men stood up from the swing seats. He advanced a few steps toward the truck and yelled something I couldn't hear through the truck window which was closed tightly. He yelled louder, "roll down the damn window!" I let it down a bit and the dogs started growling. The men on the swings set their beer cans down and started laughing.

The man with the scraggly beard moved a bit closer and yelled, "whaddya want?"

"Call off the damn dogs!" I yelled through the crack in the window. "I want some sawmilling."

Nothing happened. I picked up the hanging basket I had thrown in the truck. "I brought the lady a plant."

This got the lady's attention. She walked out to the truck, picking up a stick on the way. She walked up to the man-eating dogs, swung at them and yelled something. They cowered and retreated. She walked up to the window. "Where'd that come from?"

"We grew it. Thought you'd like it."

She came up to the window and peered in. "That's a angel wing begonia," she observed, "but I ain't seen one with that kind of bloom before."

I told her that Jerry had sent us and he had told me she liked plants.

She hesitated. "Where'd you get that plant?"

"I grew it."

"What's your name?"

"John."

"I heard about a guy they call 'John the plant man.'"

"That's me."

She turned toward the swings and yelled, "it's ok. This here is John the plant man."

I rolled the window down a bit more and handed the plant out.

I never took my eyes off the dogs. The lady followed my gaze and laughed. "It's ok. Them dogs won't hurt you. They just look mean. They might lick you to death. You can get out."

The bearded guy, who I took to be "Harce," walked slowly toward the truck drinking his beer and smoking what I assumed was a cigarette. I slowly got out of the truck, watching the dogs all the time. He walked around to the back of the pickup. "That ain't bad cedar. Where'd you get it?"

"The trees came down in the storm. I cut them to nine foot lengths."

"Got any more?"

"Maybe about ten or twelve more. I haven't cut them all up yet."

He walked around, picked up the end of one log, checked them for straightness, ran his hands over the bark and observed. "That's some of the finest cedar I ever seen."

I got out of the truck and walked around to join him.

He stroked his beard. I observed, "you must be Harce."

He looked at me for a while and said, "who told you how to say my name?"

"Jerry, over in the village."

"You a friend of his?"

"Sort of."

"That's good enough. Jerry ain't got nothing but 'sort of' friends. I'll cut the cedar on halves."

I looked at him. "I kind of wanted to know what you would charge. I really want as much of the lumber as I can get."

"I'll cut it on halves. I need the wood for my kitchen."

"That's it?"

He smiled. "That's it. You can take the deal and come have a beer or you can drive on out."

It seemed to me like a good time to go have a beer.

I grabbed a couple of beers from the cooler, told Marsha to come on, and we walked over to the pergola and I found a seat on one of the swings while Marsha went off with Harce's lady to look at the plants in the yard. Redneck women love their plants.

I was introduced to Kickstand, Boogerman, Hotshot and Jeremy.

They didn't say much. They were too busy drinking beer and rolling joints. Boogerman passed me a joint. I declined. He looked at me with a scowl on his face. "Don't smoke dope?"

I grinned. "I had to stop. It interferes with my beer drinking."

That answer seemed to suffice. Kickstand laughed.

Harce grabbed a fresh can of beer from the well-stocked cooler, taking a hit from the joint and popping the top at the same time. "We're cooking a hog," he observed. "You ever cook a hog?"

I thought about it. "No, I never cooked a whole hog."

"We been telling stories." This got my attention. I had been collecting redneck stories for years.

Harce paused, turned his beer up and looked at me for a long while.

"You know any stories? We done told every story we know."

I told Harce that we needed to unload the logs and I should leave. Harce stared at me once again.

"You kin pull over there and unload the logs, or you kin tell a story and if it's any good, we'll go unload the logs for you."

That sounded like a deal. I had always been able to tell a pretty good story and my beer buzz was in just the right place to do a good job of it. I walked over to the car and got two cans of beer.

Harce stared again. "Is this going to be a two beer story?"

"I don't know, we'll see."

chapter 4

STORIES

"My Dad never allows a few facts to get in the way of a good story"
-Paul Schulz

The situation at Harce's house was exactly what I loved to find. Any time you get around rednecks, beer, and barbecue, you run into redneck stories.

I had loved stories from the day I was born. My mother told me that she tried singing to me that day but ended up telling me a story. I was the first born to a southern lady who didn't like to be cold. She married a man from Milwaukee, had me and lived there for a while. She later told me that a man could marry a northern girl and live anywhere, but if he married a southern girl, he would sooner or later have to move south.

Mother said that she and I spent the cold winter days indoors. She passed the time telling me stories and reading to me, and the habit continued after everyone came to their senses and the family moved south. As I grew up, I became an avid reader. I ended up reading everything from Dostoyevsky to Mark Twain to the label on the toilet paper package. I even wondered why they didn't print short stories on the separate sheets of toilet paper. That way, you could read a story every morning and then use it for other things. I found reading materials everywhere. I always loved a good story. Fortunately, my formative years were well on their way before a television entered the house. I liked to read stories, listen to them, and, later on, tell them.

I learned to put my soul into telling a story, giving all I had to make a story live. I tried to tell a story with a small factual base, embellish it, add bold lies to it, ad lib, make people laugh or cry, finish up with a good punch line, and feel sure that my audience had enjoyed it fully. And when I did that – when I did a good job of telling a good story – and a listener asked, "was that true?" that made me happy. That was my goal. It was the same thing as when Swift's readers thought *Gulliver's Travels* was a true story.

I guess I discovered redneck stories in Athens, Georgia while fumbling through an English degree at the state university. Our wonderful government had made it possible for me to drink and to vote at the ripe old age of 18. That was how they justified sending young men to Vietnam. This meant that I was legally able to drink beer in the redneck bars that abounded in the Georgia countryside in the late sixties. I listened. I drank beer and I listened.

By the time I entered my late forties and met Harce, I was well-known for being able to tell a story. I was also well-known for being a heavy drinker. But the stories? I had gotten to the point where I could reach into my inventory of plots, subplots, twists and curls, and humor and pathos, twisting them through a redneck theme and *tell* a story.

And when I showed up at the sawmill at The Colons,

When I found rednecks drinking beer and cooking a hog,

Rednecks who didn't have cable or antenna television reception,

Rednecks who loved a good story,

My friend, I was ready for that day. I think my delivery that day was one of my best performances ever. I told that story.

I told them about Boots. I never knew anyone named Boots, but I told the story anyway.

I leaned back in the swing, can of beer in one hand and cigarette in the other. I was in my element. I took a swig from the beer can. I took a long pull on my cigarette. I looked each of the men in the eye silently, grinning. I pointed my first two fingers which held the cigarette at the group of them and said, "it goes like this here." (Thank you, David Allen Coe.)

"In the summer of 1961, when I was sixteen years old, I went to work for the Columbus, Georgia public works department. I was handed a swingblade and put on a road and cemetery crew. We worked side by side with the convicts from the Columbus Stockade. You've probably heard *The Columbus Stockade Blues.* That's the place.

"I worked for nine hours a day in the valley heat, swinging with a studied rhythm. It was easy. You just threw your head out of gear and thought about other things as your arm moved. As soon as the line bosses recognized the depth of my sterling character, I was promoted to 'equipment operator.' This meant that I operated a bush hog.

"In the summers of 1961 and 62, I was given the job of driving a dump truck for the meanest supervisor in the department. He was old, scrawny, and wrinkled. His name to his face was Mist' Lewis, but behind his back, he was referred to as 'Skin.'

"I started the morning by gassing up the truck at 7:00 a.m. and taking a red ticket to the ice man who gave me a 50 pound block of his product to chop up and put into the wooden keg on the front of the World War II vintage REO truck. If I didn't do it exactly right, the ice melted before 4:30 and I caught hell. At exactly 7:45, I helped Skin climb into the truck, where he would spend the day. (If he had to relieve himself, I had to move the truck to a private place.) Seven or eight black laborers jumped on the back of the truck with their swing blades and pitch forks as we drove out the gate and headed toward the stockade.

"We arrived at the stockade at 8:00 sharp, and were joined, in caravan fashion, by a van full of convicts. Skin told me where to go, and we headed for the day's work assignment. Sometimes the job was cleaning up a cemetery (where the convicts had fun as they caught the male rats, castrated them, and set them free); and sometimes it was attacking an overgrown section of Victory Drive or Pine Mountain Road. The assignments were so poorly organized that wherever we went was extremely overgrown and quite a job to clean up. The temperature was always 100 degrees or more.

"The black men made quite an impact on my teenaged Southern mind. I still remember Joe Sam, who hit a rhythm early in the day with his swingblade and sang every one of Nat King Cole's songs— sounded just like him. Foots was another. He had the largest stomach I had ever seen on a working man and he grunted as he wielded the pitchfork and steadily threw the brush from Joe Sam's swingblade onto the truck as I maneuvered it alongside. Foots spent a lot of time trying to get someone to bet with him, saying that he had a tuft of hair on the very end of his sexual apparatus. I lost 50 cents the very first day. The men were delightful and full of life as they worked their way through the nine hour days. These men supported rather large families on 75 cents an hour. No benefits.

"The convicts were another story. They were white guys. This was before the jails were integrated. They wore the regulation dirty white shirts and pants with blue stripes. They came and they went. The convicts were very happy to be able to work outside for twenty five cents a day. I feel that it did them good. I got to talk with many of them over the time I spent as 'Skin's boy' and I remember them as one of the most agreeable and pleasant groups of people I ever met.

"But, most of all, I remember the convict, Boots. Boots was a hopeless alcoholic and a peerless philosopher. He knew his Bible, too. He could quote scripture all day long. I first saw him on a Monday morning and I watched as he carefully picked up a pint liquor bottle from the side of Victory Drive, where he was cleaning up trash. He studied the flask carefully, smiled, and put it in his pocket. All week long, I watched Boots as time and again, he picked up a discarded liquor bottle, studied it, and dumped the leftover drop or two into his pocket flask. Every once in a while a little beer also found its way into his pocket stash. At lunch, Boots always made sure that I got a good helping of the navy beans and fatback that he served everybody out of the covered galvanized bucket that came with the van. When the mill whistle blew at 3:30, Boots would come and stick the bottle under the driver's seat of the dump truck, wink at me, and say, "you watch that for me, Mist' John, and keep your mouth shut, y'hea?" The flask disappeared every Friday evening.

"Boots made his thirty-day stay in the stockade, and I thought I would never see him again. I was amazed the following Monday to see him jump on the back of the dump truck with Foots and Joe Sam, laughing and joking. Boots was the first truly racially-unbiased, southern white man I had ever met. I have only met a few since.

"Boots worked steadily in the humid valley heat, keeping up with Foots and Joe Sam, often requesting Cole songs which Joe Sam freely provided. This lasted for two weeks. The flask ritual never changed. I never mentioned the flask to Boots, because I realized that there were some things that weren't talked about.

"As an equipment operator, I was not furnished with a swing blade and was therefore able to spend a lot of time watching the work being done. Boots picked up the trash. Skin said he was the best trash-picker upper in the business. I asked Boots about it at lunch one day.

"'Well, Mist' John, them folks in the stockade ain't got nothin' to smoke. These rich people that drive by keep on throwin' out half smoked cigarettes. I get 'em all. I know I can trust you so I'll tell you about it. I wrap the cigarette butts in the left over wax paper from lunch. The clean-up guy at the stockade, he gets a part of the tobacco for smugglin' it in. Then we all clean it up and roll it into cigarettes. That way, everybody in the whole jail gets to smoke. Ain't none of us got no money, so it sure does help.'

"The following Monday, Boots did not appear. I turned to Skin and asked, 'Mist' Lewis, is Boots coming back?'

"Skin thought for a moment and replied, 'Best worker I ever saw. He's good for the crew. Keeps everybody moving. You watch him. He even picks up all the cigarette butts. He don't miss nothin'. He just has a problem every six weeks. Look for him Wednesday.' That constituted two day's conversation for Skin.

"Sure enough, Boots showed up on Wednesday. He showed up on the stockade truck. He had worked two weeks, drawn his pay, got drunk and bought drinks for everybody in every bar he could find, and gotten thrown in jail for thirty days. I asked him about it.

"'Well, Mist' John, you got to work two weeks to get paid. That ain't easy for me. I ain't got no place to stay, and all my friends are in jail, except for Foots and Joe Sam. The way things are with whites and coloreds, I cain't go visit them. So I make my two weeks of hard time, get drunk, get in jail, and I got a place to stay. I got friends. Mr. Skin, he always tells the guard to get me on his crew 'cause I always work so hard for him. It ain't a bad life.'

"At the end of the final summer, knowing that it was my last day on the job and that I wouldn't be back, I had one last compelling question to ask Boots. I approached him while he was eating his beans and cornbread.

"'Hey, Boots, I got one last question for you.'

"We snuck off to the side. He looked at me kind of funny. 'Whatcha want to know?'

"'I've watched you get butts for two years. You've told me how you get them in and process them. You said y'all ain't got no money. Where do you get the rolling papers?'

"Boots gave me a sideways grin. 'That's the fun part. We cut up the pages from the Bible that the Baptists give us. This week, we're working on *The Second Epistle to the Thessalonians*. It's real interesting.

We read each paper out loud before we roll it. Passes the time.'

"'But,' I asked, 'what happens when you use up all of the pages?'

"'Then we play odd man out until we pick out which of us will be next to find Jesus. The preacher will bring him a new Bible the next day and then we start all over with Genesis. It takes a long time to smoke up a whole Bible.'"

chapter 6 BARBECUE

I had finished the story. There was a silence. Then, to my astonishment, Harce and his friends jumped up and gave me a standing ovation.

"We ain't heard a story like that one in a long time!" Harce yelled. He turned to his friends. "We'd best go unload them cedar logs. A deal is a deal." He grinned and shook my hand. Marsha had rejoined us about halfway through the story and Harce told her to back the truck down behind the barn where the sawmill stood. The men all took the time to grab a beer and light another joint. They followed slowly.

I walked around to the back of the barn and discovered a mountain of sawdust which, it turned out, hid a shed which housed the sawmill. I was amazed. There, shining in the afternoon sun, stood a saw blade. Not just any saw blade, either. This looked exactly like a blade that one would find on a skill saw but it was taller than I am. I am slightly over six feet.

Harce got a smile on his face, walked over to the blade and started wiping the dust off with an oily rag. Actually, he didn't wipe it with the rag, he caressed it. He touched it in a sensual manner like another man might reserve for making love to a woman. He paused and stared at the blade with a look of love on his face and then turned to the other men. "Put them logs over here." he ordered. It was not a request. I found out why it took four of them to unload the truck. They never set their cans of beer down. Each of them worked with only one hand, but they did it with perfect coordination. They had obviously had a lot of practice working one-handed.

"I got this here saw mill with the money I got when my grandma died." Harce told me. "It's got a seven foot blade with a Cummings diesel engine. This thing will cut a tree with a three foot diameter right down the middle." While he was telling me this, he picked up a metal detector and ran it all over the cedar logs. "In case of nails," he observed. "They tear the hell out of the blade."

I made a show of admiring something I knew absolutely nothing about. Harce was pleased.

It was getting late and we told Harce that we had to go feed the livestock which included five cats, four dogs, birds, and fish. Kickstand had remembered that he had a Gideon Bible in the glove box of his truck. He told us he had 'borried' it from a motel in Plainville. He and Jethro had torn out a page and were rolling a joint with their newly found information. Harce made a show of taking a fork and pulling a large hunk of perfectly cooked meat from the shoulder of the spread-eagled hog. He wrapped it in wax paper and tied it up with baling twine.

"I'll get that wood cut in a couple days," he said. "You come back, hea? And bring me another story, hea?"

I left the logs, took the barbecue and went home. On the way home, Marsha told me about the five foot square picture window that looked out over the mountain – a perfectly engineered view from the seat in the outhouse. She raved about the outhouse.

"Everything," she said, "is notched and pegged and sanded and varnished. There's a lavatory with a hand pump and pictures of flowers on the wall. The view is magnificent." Marsha had been in many an outhouse in her life, but she observed that "this one was the finest ever."

chapter 7
ANYTHING WITH WOOD

A couple of weeks after the visit to the saw mill, Ponytail showed up at my house. I don't know Ponytail's real name. I never did. I guess the only times I ever saw him was when he brought me a message from Harce. Ponytail always drove a partly dented black Chevy S-10. I saw him off and on for ten years, and I don't see how it could have been the same truck, but it was always a black Chevy S-10.

Ponytail was a small man. He was about five feet and six inches tall. Skinny but not too skinny, he always had a smile on his face, and he was always in a hurry. The part of Ponytail that distinguished him from anyone else in the world was the top of his head. The front part of his head was bald – not a little bit bald – totally, polished bald. It looked like someone had drawn a line across his head from ear to ear and put hair on the backside and nothing up front but skin. The hair on the backside of his head was grown out to about two feet long and worn in a tightly pulled back pony tail. It was a grey ponytail. When he talked, he stuttered and he moved his head from side to side and waved his hands around. The grey ponytail flew from one side to the other. I referred to him as "Ponytail" because I was never told anything else. After a while, everyone in The Colons picked up the name.

Ponytail drove up into the parking area at my house, jumped out of the truck, waved his hands around, grinned and asked, "A a a a re y y y y ou jjjj jjjj jjohn ththe plant m m m man?"

I answered, "that's what a lot of people call me."

He waved his hands, moved his head from side to side, and said, "w w w well, Hhh hh Harce w w w wwants y y you to come g g g get y y yyour l l lumber." He grinned and waved, got in the black Chevy S-10 and drove off. Since it was a Sunday afternoon, and since I usually kept Sunday afternoons open for drinking beer and anything else I could think of to do, I decided to ride on up to The Colons.

One requirement for visiting rednecks in Georgia on Sunday is to take your own beer. The only way to buy beer on Sunday is to get it from a bootlegger and that is expensive. Most bootleggers double their money. Everybody tries to stock up on beer for Sunday, but they often drink it all up on Saturday night. At the time, I was always careful to keep my "Sunday stash" safe and sound, keeping enough for my drinking habits, perhaps a few cans to share, but not much extra.

So, I called Marsha to drive, loaded a cooler with twelve cans of beer – enough for me and some to share – one must be polite. I picked up a blooming trailing red rose to take to Louann and we headed off to see what the afternoon would bring. The trip was uneventful and we pulled up on the exact same scene as the first time except the dogs seemed to accept us, Harce waved, and two of the men on the swing were passed out with their heads lolled back, rolling around with the movement of the swing.

I got out of the truck, handed Harce a beer and grabbed one for me. He told Marsha to drive around behind the sawmill as he and I walked. When we went around the corner of the barn, I saw two neat stacks of lumber that looked exactly the same.

Harce looked up at me. "When I was a kid and we had a candy bar, one kid got to divide it up and the other one got to choose which half he wanted. Grandma said that way it would be even."

He pointed at the lumber. "I divided it into two piles. There's one-by-sixes, one- by-fours, a couple of two-by-eights, a couple two-by-fours, and some one by tens that will bring tears to a carpenter's eyes."

He held up a piece with bark on it. "These here are the slabs from the outside of the log. I use them for birdhouses and the scraps for kindling."

He stood back and waved his arm down like a Baghdad cloth merchant. "You choose your pile."

I took a minute to look at each pile. I kept my hands in my pockets. "Tell you what, Harce, you choose my pile."

He gave me a studious, funny look. "That ain't fair, John"

"Harce, please, please tell me why it is not fair for you to divide it and for you to pick my stack, I really don't understand."

"Well, see, John." He raised his hands over his shoulders with his palms up in a manner that was almost a prayer and almost a "what the hell"—"See, John, I told you what Grandma taught me about dividing. Now you're making me go to what Grandpa taught me about dividing."

He pointed at each stack of wood. "One of them two stacks is better than the other. I know which one it is. If you pick the stack you want, I stand a seventy-thirty chance of getting the best one 'cause you don't know nothing about it. According to Grandpa before he died, if I pick your stack then I'm honor-bound to give you the best one."

I watched as he studied the stacks of wood, wondering how it would turn out.

"Tell you what." He pointed to a stack. "I'm gonna give you that one on the left. Pull the truck up."

I grinned and said, "I think I really want the one on the right. That way if you were really giving me the best stack, you will be rewarded for honesty. If you weren't, you will learn."

Harce grinned. "You really don't give a damn one way or the other, do you?"

"Naw," I replied. We both laughed.

We loaded the lumber and then popped us open another can of beer.

Harce took a long swig, wiped his mouth with the back of his hand and observed, "You're kind of different. I ain't met nobody like you."

I took this as a compliment, considering the source. "Thank you."

He took another swig of beer, wiped his mouth with the back of his hand, and asked, "You want to see my house? I don't usually show it to most folks. Built it myself."

And after the outhouse report from Marsha on our last trip, I really did want to see the house. I had studied the house from a distance and it looked to be a different sort of log cabin comprising maybe fifteen hundred to two thousand square feet. It had a welcoming front porch with a tin roof and it might have been a lot like several other log houses I had seen. But it wasn't.

As we walked up beside the house, I stopped and admiringly ran my hand across a piece of the lumber. Harce watched.

"Them's red oak ten-by-tens. Hand-sanded, rubbed with ten coats of linseed oil. Louann buffed it by hand." That was the first time I had seen anything like this and it was the first time Harce had mentioned a real name for his "old lady." I found out later that when she had done something that really pleased him, she was "Louann." Any other time she was "the old lady."

I walked to the corner of the house and studied the joints. You couldn't slide a piece of paper between them. Harce grinned proudly. "I cut the ten-by-tens from a bunch of trees I got at a place they bulldozed for a road cut. I cut the joints with a hand saw and did the first smoothing with a draw knife."

I looked closely and remarked, "I don't see any nail heads."

"It's all notched and pegged. There ain't a nail in it."

We walked on. I stopped dead still at the door. I put my hands on it gently and looked at him with my eyebrows up. "Walnut?"

"Yeah," he grinned. "This doctor paid me to take the tree out of his yard. He didn't like the leaves in the fall. I cut it up in my sawmill."

I reached up and touched the curved molding over the half round top of the door.

"Hand carved," he replied. "Grandpa used to make such as that on winter nights while Grandma knitted. That's when I learned to like wood."

We walked in and I looked at the floors.

"That's hundred year old heart pine I got from when they tore down the cotton mill. They paid me to haul it off. I planed it and sanded it."

Then I looked up and studied everything around me. It seemed as we talked, that Harce had never spent any money on any part of the house. It was built of items that he had cut in the sawmill, that he had found in the woods, on the side of the road, or God knows where, or that someone had "paid him to haul off." The house was an amazing piece of work. The kitchen walls were of polished cedar, the cabinets hand-crafted from white oak. The kitchen counters were made of cast-off pieces of tile with inlays showing different trees with birds, deer, dogs, and cats.

In the living room, standing like an altar, was a large, polished wood heater with a fire crackling inside. "That's the only thing I didn't make," he observed. "I'm going to make me a wood heater one day. I can make one better."

I asked, "Harce, do you ever waste any part of a tree?"

He thought about it. "I don't reckon we do. We get lumber, firewood, kindling, and we mix the sawdust and leaves with cow manure to make compost for the garden. No, I don't reckon we do."

All my life I had appreciated and paid attention to good wood crafting, but there was too much of it in Harce's house for me to see in one visit. All of the furniture was handmade except for the recliner which—yep, he had "been paid to haul off." I didn't see every part of the house because, "Louann don't want you to see the bedroom." He never said why.

Marsha and Louann had finished planting the rose bush. I passed out cans of beer to anyone still sober enough to drink one and we went on home. Louann had sent a quart jar of Brunswick stew for our dinner. It was really good. I wondered what was in it.

chapter 8 THE GREENHOUSE

There was always some disagreement as to whether the lake was the front yard or the back yard. It's a nice lake and the house is between it and the road. We just kind of used it as the front yard and so I called it that. Marsha's grandfather had built the lake in the early fifties and she kind of grew up there and inherited it later on. She had spent years cleaning out weeds, vines, and snakes from around the lake. We had worked together to install rock gardens and sitting areas in strategic locations and there were flowers, sitting stumps, and shade trees. I had given her a Japanese maple for each of her last five birthdays. These were given places of honor in the overall lakescape. It was called "Catfish Heaven" thanks to my brother who said that this was where "catfish went when they died." I always said that if I died and was reincarnated, I wanted to come back as one of Marsha's cats. Her cats had a good life.

I will never forget one beautiful, late spring Sunday afternoon. Marsha was working in her raised vegetable garden on one edge of the lake. I had been really turned on by Harce's wood work and I was working outside, building a hand-crafted kitchen table. I was working with the beautiful cedar one-by-tens that we had gotten a few weeks before, sanding the wood and fitting it with a white oak inlay. The table was to be Marsha's birthday present in May. It ended up being her Christmas present. Oh, well.

I stopped and cocked my head as I heard a truck coming up the road. I guess the truck might have had a half a muffler. Maybe less. It turned into our gravel driveway at the bottom of the hill and the dogs started barking and raising hell. I grabbed my beer can and looked around the corner of the house to see an old, white, wrinkled pickup truck bouncing up the hill. I say "white" but that was just the original color, I guess. One door was red and one front fender was brown. A chunk of the bed on the passenger's side was rusted out. The bed was filled with fishing rods and some kind of tanks sticking up. I don't think any two of the tires were the same size.

Marsha called the dogs off. Louann climbed out through the window on the passenger's side, Harce opened the driver's door, stepped out, stretched with his hands over his head, drained his can of beer, threw it in the back of the truck, yelled, "Louann, get me a beer," and looked around until he saw me. "Louann's got a notion to go fishing," he allowed.

I soon found out that it was a twofold visit. Louann wanted to go fishing. Harce wanted to get into my stash of Sunday beer. It was all right, though, because it was one of those rare Sundays when I had both of my coolers full.

After looking around a little while, Louann went fishing on the dock, Marsha went back to her vegetable garden, I picked up my sandpaper and Harce got a beer and pulled up a chair so he could give his undivided attention to telling me exactly what I was doing wrong with the table.

I worked a while. He told me how to do the job for a while. I began thinking that perhaps I would do well to find some way to spend my Sunday afternoon that would be better than getting woodworking instructions. It was kind of like two little boys having a pissing contest.

I stood and stretched. "I'm building a greenhouse. You want to see it?"

That got his attention. I found, over time, that if I wanted to get Harce's attention, all I had to do was say something with the word "build" in it. He brightened up.

I pointed. "It's up there on the hill." Harce grinned, stuffed a can of beer in each of his jacket pockets and replied, "Let's go see it."

I was right proud of my greenhouse. I had designed a modified "A" frame, devised a bending jig and had formed and erected all of the arches. It was all made of electrical conduit. There was a pile of pipes sitting in front of it that were to be used for connecting the arches. Harce was impressed. I remember thinking, "all right, sumbitch, tell me how to do this one better."

He walked around looking, studying. He grabbed a level that was laying around and checked one of the walls. He smiled and nodded. My day immediately got better.

Then he looked at the connecting strips.

"How you going to attach these?" He took a swig of beer.

"I was planning to use U bolts. But none of the hardware stores had enough of them the right size. I've got them on order."

He looked at the pile of pipe. "Going to take a bunch of them."

"Yeah," I replied, "a hundred and seventy five."

"That's a lot of money."

"You said that right." I thought and calculated. "About a dollar and a half apiece."

"That's a lot of beer." Harce always thought of expenditures in comparison to the price of beer.

He walked around and pondered. "You want me to help you fix it?"

"I don't have the U bolts," I replied. "I already told you that."

He pointed at the house. "Don't need no U bolts. Go get me a bunch of coat hangers."

I looked at him. "You can't tie them up with coat hangers. The joint has to be tight and perfectly spaced."

Harce quietly sipped his beer. He didn't like to be argued with. "Go get some damn coat hangers."

I thought, "OK, asshole, I'll go get the coat hangers and watch you mess it up." I didn't say anything, though, thankfully. I just slowly walked to the house and did as I was told. This was how I learned that when I was around Harce, and when it came to building, I could save myself a lot of embarrassment if I kept my mouth shut.

When I returned from my errand with a bunch of coat hangers, I saw that Harce had driven his truck up the hill and was moving one of the tanks over to the greenhouse frame. I watched as he found my marks and clamped a ten foot piece of connecting pipe in place.

"That where you want it?"

"It's perfect," I replied.

Harce walked to the truck and got a welding helmet, put it on his head, grabbed a coat hanger from me, cut a strip of it with a pair of pliers, put on a pair of serious leather gloves, picked up his welding torch and said, "don't look at the burn." He held the coat hanger at the joint of the pipe and applied the torch. He stood back, raised the helmet visor and examined the weld. He lowered the visor and quickly touched up a place. He repeated the process on two more of the arches and was finished with the section. He took off his helmet. "That's how you do it."

I was amazed. "Will it hold?"

"Hell, yeah, it'll hold. You can do pull-ups on that pipe and it won't move."

He wiggled the pipe, showing me how sturdy the construction was. I had lost the pissing contest, but I really didn't care. I was impressed. I was happy. Now we could finish the greenhouse. I told Harce how impressed I was.

He finished off his beer, threw the can toward the garbage can, pulled another from his pocket, opened it and asked, "how much do them U bolts cost?"

"I think about a dollar and a half plus tax."

He counted the four welds. "Lookee there. That's two six packs. Give me another pipe."

I slowly set down my beer can and just as slowly headed for the stack of pipe.

"Hurry the hell up," he yelled. "You want to finish this today or not?"

Then he turned and yelled down the hill, "Louann, bring us some beer." Louann immediately set her fishing pole down and headed for the cooler.

Harce worked my ass off. My job was to hand him pipe, mark the locations for the welds, keep him supplied with coat hanger pieces, clamp the pipe in place, and keep a beer in his hand. The greenhouse was fifty feet long and that meant twenty five arches with four runners and diagonals to be welded. That's a lot of welds. Harce would make four welds and holler, "there's another six pack." When we ran short of beer, Harce yelled at Louann who brought four cans at the time, three for Harce and one for me.

I occasionally looked up and watched the sun moving slowly toward the western sky. I hauled pipe, clamped, opened beer cans, and did everything else he told me to do. Keep in mind, he didn't "ask" me to do anything. He "told" me to do it. There's a big difference. Harce didn't know how to ask. We got close to the end of the job as the sun set. Harce didn't let that stop him. He turned the truck around and we put the last 6 joints together by the light of the truck's left headlight. The right headlight didn't work.

I don't know who was more proud of the job. Harce for showing me how to do it, or me for having it done. To me, this meant that I could put the plastic cover over the frame and we could begin growing our bedding plants and flowers. To Harce, it meant another job well done, it meant that he had beat me on my turf, and it meant something else I learned about later. That something else was called "payback." We packed up and headed down to the house.

Harce allowed that it was time to relax and drink a beer. The evening was getting cool and Marsha had started a fire in the wood heater. Four potatoes were nestled in the coals to bake. We pulled up chairs around the fire. Harce called, "Louann, bring us a beer, then filet four of them bass you caught and we'll see if John can cook them on the grill." Louann quickly did as told. Beer first, fish second. I clamped the filets in a fish basket and put them in the freezer for five minutes to get cool. Then I poured melted butter over them, watching the butter congeal as it hit the cold fish. I sprinkled a bit of seasoning over the tops and stuck them directly over the coals in the wood heater, closing the door. Harce grinned. "I just learnt something about cooking fish." Marsha and Louann made a salad.

What a day. The greenhouse was done, I had a new friend, I was pleasantly tired and I felt good after having stuffed myself with a wonderful fish dinner. I leaned back in the chair with a smile on my face. "I guess I owe you for the work," I observed.

"Yeah, you do," he replied. "Louann, get me another one of John's beers, then come in here, he's going to tell us a story."

That suited me. I knew exactly which one of my stories I would tell. Harce needed to hear the one about Shorty in Phenix City. I thought Louann would enjoy it as well.

chapter

9

SHORTY

Harce and Louann pulled up chairs to listen. Marsha had heard the story before and started cleaning up the kitchen. Harce popped the top on a beer. I leaned back and started the narrative:

"I had met Shorty in a bar outside of Phenix City, Alabama in 1970. Actually, it was more than a bar. The sign outside read, 'JR's Bar and Grill and Bait Store.'

"You had to leave Columbus, Ga., go through Phenix City and turn left toward Eufaula. The landmark for a left turn onto an unmarked road was a 'Land For Sale' sign on the right which had been there forever because the land was so sorry nobody wanted to buy it even for a trailer lot. Then you had to go up the hill, left up a dirt drive, and try to find a place to park wherever you could. The parking lot was fluid and never in the same place from one time to the next. Someone would dump an old motor or transmission in part of the "parking lot" and Junior, the owner, would come out with his end loader and push up older, already-pirated stuff for another parking lot.

"Depending on where the parking lot was, a rocky clay pathway meandered up through the weeds, beer cans, and truck parts to a building that had started off as a pole barn which got closed in and then got a cement floor poured through the window and then was added on to again in the same manner. Junior bought the chairs and tables at a going-out-of-business sale for the Pentecostal church that took out a loan for electric fans because God didn't want them to have air conditioning. Apparently, God didn't want them to have fans, either. So, all the chairs had 'property of Third Pentecoastal Church of the Rapture' stenciled on their backs. He got a couple of the fans, too.

"The main barn was the bar, with a linoleum covered counter, eight tables, more or less, and twenty-four chairs more or less. The count on chair legs varied. Three two gallon jars sat on the bar holding pickled eggs, pickled sausages, and jalapeno peppers. Junior's most prized possession stood at the end of the bar under a spotlight—a bright, shiny Wurlitzer juke box. Junior had gone to a lot of trouble to have the right records installed—everything Hank Williams had ever written or sung, three or four George Jones songs, and a little Buddy Holly. Junior said that Hank was the only really good, timeless singer, George Jones was a very special drunk, and Buddy Holly was there to piss off the hippies.

"Crickets, catawba worms, red wigglers, and minnows were ordered up and sold over the bar. They were passed through the window from the next room by whoever was 'mechaniking' in the shop. Shorty, the bartender, would dip a rag in Go Jo and wipe the grease off of the bait containers before passing them over the bar. I always wondered what the sweet, prim lady at the bank thought when she had to count the money when Junior made a deposit—if he ever did make one.

"I once asked Junior if JR stood for his name, like Joe Roscoe or something and he said, "naw, it stands for Junior. My maw and paw couldn't figure out how to spell junior, so Paw finally got mad and wrote JR. Then, when we started painting the sign, we tried to figure out how to spell it and six people came up with seven different ways to spell it so I just said screw it, put JR up there.

"Hank Williams seemed to crawl in the window as Shorty slowly picked up the church key, wiped it with his GoJo rag and popped a top from the bar bottle of Black Label.

Pick guitar, fill fruit jar, and be gayo

Son of a gun, we'll have big fun on the bayou.

"'Tell you what,' said Shorty. 'I never really thought I would be serving beer to people for a living. I kind of had it going pretty good and then everything went to hell and I guess I got kind of low and lost my job and here I am.'

"I just formed what I thought was a quizzical look with my eyebrows and kept my mouth shut.

"'I was a welder, you see,' he continued, wiping the bar off with his Go Jo rag and then wiping off the Go Jo with a blue gas station paper towel. 'Man, I had it made. I was welding pretty steady at the paper mill, been welding for a goodly number of years. Been living with the old lady for seven or eight years and we had this nice trailer in the Azalea Garden mobile home park up on the four-lane. Never could figure it out. There weren't no garden and there couldn't have been no azalea cause they had pulpwooded it right before we moved in and there weren't nothing there but pine tree stumps.

"'It was nice, though. The old lady liked flowers, and she had her pots of hens and chicks on one stump and her begonias on another stump. I drilled a hole in one of the stumps and put up one of them beach umbrellas and we had some chairs and a garbage can to put the beer cans in. I built a stoop out of some concrete blocks and fixed a pen in the back for Rocky, he's my bird dog.

"'Anyway, I was working pretty long hours. Maybe five in the morning to six at night. Made pretty good money, though. I got her a '55 Chevy Bel Air. Blue and white it was, with a nice six cylinder in it that I knew she weren't going to get no speeding ticket with. She used to bitch all the time, though, when it rained, because the windshield wipers ran off the vacuum and when you pushed on the gas, the wipers would stop moving.

"'You had to take off your shoes too, before you went in the house when it rained, because that red mud was like glue, and you couldn't even scrape it off on the concrete blocks.

"'I even used to take her out to eat on Sunday afternoons. I thought I treated her pretty good. Even after Krystals went up to twelve cents, I would take her in and sit at the bar in the restaurant with her and tell her to get all she wanted. Bought her a large coke, too. And French fries. Then, we'd go to the bootleggers and pick up some Black Labels because they don't let you buy beer on Sunday except at the bootleggers, and I would get some and go put it in the ice box and watch the ball game. She was nice, too. I'd say "hey babe, get me a beer" and she'd bring me one and pop the top with the churchkey and take my empty bottle and go pick up her book and read some more until I needed another one. I had it made pretty good, and I didn't have to cut no grass, neither.

"'Then, after a year or two, she started getting quiet. She didn't want to go dancing anymore. I didn't know what was wrong with her and I thought she just had the mopes. I guess that's when I messed up. I told her we really didn't need the money, but maybe she ought to get a job to get her out of the house and give her something to do.'

"Shorty stopped talking to me while he opened a couple of Black Labels for some new arrivals, yelled through the window to the mechanic for a tube of crickets, fished me out a pickled egg, slid the bottle of Tabasco and a pack of saltines down the bar, rang up everybody's money on the crank handle cash register, and sauntered over to where I sat, washing down egg yolk and Tabasco with my cold Black Label. I thought, *efficiency like that is hard to find.*

"'Well, she got a part time job stocking the shelves down at the ten cent store. She didn't make much money, but it gave her something to do. Thing that bothered me, though, she kept getting quieter and quieter. Even with her job, she was still home when I left and home when I got back. She got where she would play possum when I got up and would act like she was asleep instead of saying goodbye.

"'Then one night, I got home, and there were these boxes all over the hall in the trailer. She was real quiet when I told her to get me a beer. Then, as she popped the top, she told me that that made the end of exactly 100 six packs of beer that she had brought me because I told her to. She asked me how many bottles of beer that was—she never was much good at arithmetic—and I told her that would be right at 600. Then she mumbled something under her breath that I didn't understand and shut herself up in the bedroom.

"'I didn't know exactly what I had done wrong, but I didn't worry much about it and I slept on the couch and got up the next morning and went to work. I did wonder about all the boxes and thought she might be thinking of moving out but I figured that would be all right, 'cause she hadn't been much fun lately anyhow.'

"He walked over to the shop window, took a carton of worms and a tube of crickets from the mechanic, wiped them off with his GoJo rag, and handed them to the fisherman by the bar, rang up the money, and brought me another Black Label.

"'Anyway, I went to work, and when I got home that night, I found out what the boxes were for.'

"It was nearing 6:00 and the bar was getting crowded. Shorty popped a bunch of tops and sold some bait and pickled eggs. The Tabasco bottle was getting a work-out. Shorty was getting a workout.

"The big Wurlitzer speakers were pounding out one of Hank's more obscure songs:

Your daddy's mad, he's done got peeved
You're gonna change
Or I'm agonna leave.

"I couldn't stand it. I had to get on the road while I could still navigate. I ordered one more Black Label.

"When he brought my beer, I said, 'So, you can't leave me there, Shorty, what were the boxes for?'

"'Oh, yeah, I forgot,' he said, wiping off his churchkey. 'The boxes were sitting there in the trailer lot with my stuff in them.'

"She put *your* stuff in them?" I asked.

"'That's right,' he replied. 'And the damn trailer was long gone, she'd had it hauled off. All that was left was my stuff in boxes and an uncapped septic tank hook-up. Never seen her since. Sure do miss old Rocky.'

"I started out the door, hesitated, turned and walked back up to the bar and asked Shorty, 'Did you ever figure out what it was that she muttered before she shut herself in her room?'

"'Something about Jesus said that was enough. I never did

get it.'"

As I finished the story, I looked up at Harce and Louann. Louann had a big grin on her face. Harce looked pensive.

Louann laughed. "I guess that taught the sumbitch," she observed. "Now, Shorty's the one getting the beer for everybody. You got that, Harce?"

Harce looked her straight in the eye. "OK, I guess I got it, Louann, I ain't never going to tell you to get me a beer again."

Louann smiled. Harce continued, "You just be sure you figure out when I want one and bring it to me."

LOUANN

Louann was a victim of numbers. With five more years of public schooling, thirty more points of I.Q., and eight more teeth, she could have been a movie star. She was all right to look at when she kept her mouth shut – which was rarely. She could also look halfway intelligent under the same circumstances. Louann could talk more and say less than any woman I had ever met. Her vocabulary was limited but she made up for it by using the word "like" and the phrase "don't you know" quite often. A sample sentence might be: "I like caught this don't you know fish and like I pulled it in out of the don't you know water and like it was slippery. You know what I mean?"

When I met her she was in her late twenties. She was about five feet six inches tall with long straight mousy brown hair which she always said used to be "you know, like it was blonde, don't you know." Louann wore cutoffs and a t-shirt in the summer and jeans and a sweatshirt in the winter. She was barefoot unless it was really cold. When it was really cold she wore work boots.

Louann was rather uncommunicative around men, so I only knew her from observation. After she got to know Marsha, though, she told Marsha everything in the world about her life, her activities, her ways of getting money, and her alcohol consumption. Marsha, of course, told me everything. It was much more than I wanted to know.

My observations were that Louann was very gentle and understanding when dealing with animals and plants. She could communicate with the animals on their level, and I once watched her squatting and staring at a tomato plant for hours. I asked her what she was doing and she replied, "I'm like watching it grow, don't you know." The dogs might have barked the first time she came to the house to go fishing, but after that, they started wagging their tails when Harce's truck pulled into the driveway. If Louann wasn't with Harce, they would bark at him, otherwise they would come sit in front of Louann and let her pet them and talk to them.

Louann helped grow Harce's animals. There were always chickens, hogs, and a cow or two around "the property." Harce and Louann never had to buy meat or vegetables. She saw to that. But she told Marsha that even though she loved watching the animals grow, she never named them because "You can, like, eat a piece of you know steak but only if you don't know any names, don't you know. It's like, you can't eat Herman, but eating a don't you know stranger is all right. See? That's like why I don't never name none of them, don't you know. See, it's all right to name a tomato plant don't you know because you are only eating their babies, don't you know and you don't name their babies. You know? I name all my tomato plants, but like, I don't never name a chicken. Not around here. You know?"

Louann was never idle. The deal on the firewood was that Harce cut and split the firewood. Louann used a hatchet to split wood scraps into kindling. Splitting kindling is a dangerous art form. Louann could patiently cut strips of wood to an amazing degree of exactness without ever cutting herself with the hatchet. She separated the kindling into two piles: hardwood and heart pine. She tied the kindling into separate bundles that were about eight inches in diameter and ten inches long. The heart pine kindling was in big demand at the Magic Market.

While Harce was away looking for any possible way to make money other than get a job, Louann kept things together at home. She grew and canned vegetables. She fed and cared for the livestock with no names. She split kindling and picked up beer cans for recycling. One of Harce's friends had built her a beer can crusher which consisted of two tires with an electric motor and a chute that fed the cans between the tires and spit them out into a barrel. There was never a shortage of beer cans around the sawmill. When Harce built the brick barbecue pit, she had him set a couple of mailboxes into the chimney. This way, when the chimney got hot, she could bake bread in the mailbox. It was the best bread anyone ever ate. She gathered eggs. She used a homemade broom to sweep the front yard, just like her mother and grandmother had done. Louann stayed busy.

Louann was a closet alcoholic. She loved to get drunk, but she had certain restrictions. You see, as much as Harce drank, he didn't like her when she was drunk. He threw violent fits when she got drunk. I guess I could understand. I only saw her really drunk twice and I really didn't want to be anywhere near her at those times. She was a wild, incomprehensible, screaming banshee when she was drunk. Obviously she knew this also and she did a really good job of getting just the right buzz and maintaining it throughout the day. She had to be very devious, though, in getting alcohol. Harce would bring her a six pack of Keystone beer every three or four days and he thought that was all she drank. She wasn't above drinking up the vanilla extract, but she didn't really like the taste.

So Louann learned to scrounge money. She couldn't drive because she got in trouble every time she tried to drive somewhere and Harce never left an operational vehicle on the premises when he was not there. If he drove off in one truck, he had the coil wire from the other truck in his pocket. But Louann could scrounge beer money better than anyone around The Colons. She sold kindling to the Magic Market, she sold eggs to the neighbors, she cheated on the recycled beer cans, she made kudzu vine wreaths at Christmas time. She was full of financial schemes – all centered on buying beer.

Since she couldn't drive, she had to share her largesse with her friend from down the road, Mary Sue, who had the use of a 1979 Chevrolet Impala that ran most of the time. For two dollars worth of gas, one can of beer, and three fresh chicken eggs, Mary Sue would drive Louann to the Magic Market whenever she wanted to go. Louann had to be careful to keep any indication that she had any money from Harce or he would take it. He knew why she wanted money. If he didn't think she had any, he would just think that she was only drinking the beer that he brought her. That's what she wanted him to think. That's kind of how she won the lottery.

Louann told Marsha about winning the lottery but swore her to secrecy. Marsha, of course, told me and swore me to secrecy. If Harce had ever known, his wrath would have been legendary. I sure as hell wasn't going to tell him. The story went like this.

I think it was Harley Johnson, I'm not sure, but it really doesn't matter, who came to see Louann to buy a piece of cured ham. She wanted five dollars for the ham but Harley only had four dollars and an unscratched lottery ticket. Louann didn't really want the lottery ticket, but Harley was nice and had a nice smile and he also threw in a can of Budweiser so she took the deal. She put the ticket in with her financial stash and forgot about it.

A couple of days later, Louann counted and found that she had saved up ten dollars. Harce was gone to cut trees so she got some eggs and walked down the road to fetch Mary Sue. They cranked the old Chevy and headed down to the Magic Market. Neither of them had drunk a beer in two days and it wasn't that they really wanted a twelve pack, they really needed a twelve pack. Louann had stuffed her money in her pocket without looking at it and when she reached in to hand Mary Sue the gas money, the lottery ticket fell out on the floor of the car.

Mary Sue looked at it. "Where did you get the lottery ticket?"

Louann told her about Harley Johnson pawning it off on her. Mary Sue was incredulous. "And you ain't scratched it yet? I ain't never known nobody that didn't scratch them even before they got out of the store." So they both huddled over the Lucky Seven card while Louann took a dime out of her pocket and scratched.

She scratched the covering off of the first block. "What is it?" asked Mary Sue.

"It's a by damn seven," Louann replied. "All we need is two more sevens. Fat chance, don't you know." She scratched another one.

Mary Sue yelled a modified rebel yell. "Look, it's another seven. Scratch the next one."

Louann hesitated. The tension built. She slowly scratched the third block. There was silence.

"It's another seven, that's three of them," Mary Sue whispered. "Scratch that box down there. That's the one that tells you what you won."

Louann scratched it.

There was dead silence.

"My God," whispered Louann

"Oh, oh my God," whispered Mary Sue.

"It's five thousand dollars," whispered Louann. "That will buy beer for the rest of my life."

"What are we going to do?"

"We can't let Harce know, he'll take it."

"We can't take it into the Magic Market. Harry will tell everybody."

"Let's buy some gas and go to town to the Indian store. He cain't tell nobody we know 'cause they won't go in there."

Louann tried for a straight face and went into the Magic Market to pay for the gas. Harry asked her about her beer, but she told him she "wouldn't be needing any today." She ran out the door.

The Chevy was still running because Louann and Mary Sue had learned not to cut it off when it was away from home. They headed into town to the Indian store, which was the largest lottery purveyor around. They ran in and set the ticket on the counter.

The clerk took the ticket and studied it carefully.

"You mus' go to Dalton for a prize this size," he observed. "Dey only let us pay out up to one t'ousand dollars here. You mus go to Dalton for dis one. Sorry."

Outside, Louann and Mary Sue huddled together. "Damn, we got to go to Dalton," Louann said.

"It's OK," said Mary Sue. "I think the Chevy will make it. It's only 70 miles. But we'll need about fifteen dollars for gas. See what you can get and I'll rob my change jar and we can go tomorrow."

Louann got up extra early the next morning and fixed a big breakfast for Harce. She wanted to get him out of there. The minute he was out of the driveway, she took off her bathrobe which covered her jeans and sweat shirt. She ran to Mary Sue's house. The Chevy was already running. They stopped at the Magic Market and bought fourteen dollars and eighty six cents worth of gas and they were off.

They only had to stop and ask directions six times, but they finally found their way to the lottery redemption office. Mary Sue gave her rebel yell and Louann's long hair flew in the wind as they ran into the office. Louann ran up to the counter and slapped the ticket down in front of a nice grey-haired, grandmotherly lady who was obviously used to excitement. The lady studied the card. She entered the serial number into the computer and got a studious look on her face.

"It looks fine, ladies." She beamed. "If you'll just let me see your driver's license, I'll do the paperwork and give you your money."

Louann looked at Mary Sue.

Mary Sue looked at Louann.

They both looked at the lady behind the counter.

"We ain't got no drivers license," Louann said.

The lottery lady gave them a sweet smile. She had seen this before. "I'm sorry. Without a driver's license, we can't honor the amount on the card. Perhaps you have a friend . . ."

Louann and Mary Sue almost cried. They went out and sat in the car.

Louann thought for a while and asked, "What are we like going to do?"

"I don't know." Mary Sue replied, "That lady said maybe if we had a friend . . ."

Louann brightened, "Like, what about Leroy? Has he got any license?"

"I know he does. He just got out of DUI school and got them back."

"Reckon he'd do it and keep his mouth shut?"

"Reckon he would for a hunnerd dollars."

"That'd be worth it. Let's go get Leroy. He lives in Sugar Hill. That ain't but twenty miles."

"I hope he's home."

"I bet he's home, he's laid off and he's getting unemployment. He's probably out of beer. He's home."

Forty-five minutes later, they pulled up to the front of Leroy's trailer. It was easy to find. It was the first trailer in the second row of the trailer park on Highway 27 in Sugar Hill. Leroy was sitting on the porch.

Louann hollered, "Hey, Leroy."

Leroy grinned and waved. "Hey Louann. Hey, Mary Sue. What y'all doing here?"

"We thought you might want some beer."

"You got that right."

"You got any drivers license?"

Leroy took a drag from his Marlboro Light. "Yeah, I got them back the other day."

"Well get them license and get in the car and we'll go get some money and we'll get you some beer and we'll give you a hunnert dollars."

Leroy really didn't understand, but he had a chance to ride around with a couple of good-looking women and he really didn't have much else to do but sit on the porch, so he got in the back seat of the Impala. They explained the situation on the way. They were careful not to tell Leroy exactly how much money was involved until they had made a deal and shook on it. Leroy said he would be happy with a hundred dollars and some beer. He didn't have nothing else to do.

Back in Dalton, the ladies grinned big as they walked in with Leroy and saw the same nice grey-haired, grandmotherly lady behind the counter. She looked at the ticket again. She punched the numbers in the computer again. She entered Leroy's driver's license number in the computer. She got a large smile on her face and said, "If you will wait a moment, Leroy, I will have a check for you. The Georgia Lottery appreciates your support." She turned to a printer which was already processing the check.

The grey-haired lady tore off the check and brought it to the counter. "Here you are, Leroy. One hundred and twenty six dollars and forty two cents. And congratulations Leroy, your child support payments have now been caught up completely."

chapter 11
WHAT IS A REDNECK?

I enjoyed working with my redneck friends because they knew how to get things done. I knew there was something different about them and their experiences that set them apart from me and the experiences of my younger days. I had pondered long and hard on the differences, asking myself, "Just what is a redneck?" One day I found the answer.

When I was in grammar school during the early 1950s in the piedmont of North Carolina, every year there would be a fall break. For me, this was a two-week period in which to play. I was told that this break was for all of the kids who lived on the farm and needed to pick tobacco. "They may as well take a break," my father told me. "Those kids are going to be in the fields one way or another." He took me to see a tobacco barn one time, too. I didn't know what was going on, but I did know I didn't want any part of it. I never really thought about the lives of my school mates. I merely figured that their lives mirrored my sheltered existence in some way. I never understood the term "redneck" until I listened to a conversation with Bud, Harce, and George.

Bud and Harce were helping me finish up the installation of a sprinkler system in George Adam's new yard. I had known George for years. He was an old country boy, maybe 65 or so at the time, who had grown up in Alabama and made it pretty good in the heating and air business in Georgia. George had a heart condition and expected to die any day, but he was always happy and he was always busy building or growing something. George had stories to tell.

My job was to put the fine tuning on the sprinkler heads, which involved adjusting the trajectory and distance while each one was running. My job on this cold spring morning involved getting wet. I adjusted the final sprinkler head to perfection and jumped back. "Whoo, that water is cold!" Bud and Harce laughed about it.

George Adams got a funny look on his face and walked over to feel the water coming out of the sprinkler. He straightened up and looked at me. "Hell, John, that water ain't cold. I'll tell you about cold water. When I was a kid, daddy always had something growing for the grocery market. In the early spring, we harvested the spring onions. When we filled the back of the pickup truck, Daddy would back it up to this spring fed creek and then he'd sit in the truck and drink his 'shine while I washed the onions in the water right where it came out of the ground. Now, that was cold water! When I got finished washing them, I had to tie the onions up into bundles of twenty and stack them neatly in the back of the truck." He paused, shaking his head slowly. "Now, that was cold water." George stood there staring off into the sky, obviously lost in the memory.

"After Daddy sobered up the next day, we took the onions over into Georgia and sold them to old Mr. Smith at the Piggly Wiggly down on Broad Street. Mr. Smith was something else. I do believe he counted every onion in each bunch. He wasn't very nice to us. We were 'rednecks' and even though he couldn't stock his store without rednecks, he didn't have to be nice to them. I remember, after he finished counting the onions, Mr. Smith would pull out his wallet and slowly count out a few bills and hand them to Daddy. Daddy held his head up and counted the bills again, even more slowly. He valued his pride. He could take whatever came his way and serve it back to the giver in turn." George gazed out over the upscale neighborhood like none of us were there. "That was some cold water."

After about a minute, George kind of came back to reality and looked around to see the three of us staring at him with our mouths open, waiting for him to continue. He definitely had everyone's attention. "Then there was the corn," he continued. "The common practice on growing corn, or what we called "roasting ears," was to plant acres and acres of the same thing at the same time. This gave a good yield and was easy to manage, but when the corn came in, you had to work your ass off harvesting it, shucking, canning, selling to the Pig, you name it. The problem was it all came in together and after you like to killed yourself with it, there wasn't any more. When there wasn't any more was when the price went up. Well, Daddy didn't like that system, so he did some research. It was a bit more trouble, but he would plant ten rows of one kind of white, ten more rows of one kind of yellow, and so on, using varieties that took different times from planting to maturity. This way, when the corn came in, we had six weeks to deal with it. And that wasn't the best part. The best part was that about three weeks into the harvest, a lot of everybody else's corn was gone and the price went up. We would take a pickup load to Mr. Smith and some more to the people at the farmer's market who played like they grew it. The farmer's market people liked Daddy's formula, too, because sometimes they would be the only ones there with roastin' ears. I remember one time . . ." He stared off in the distance. We lost him again. Finally, Bud cleared his throat and George started up again.

"One time, we took a bunch of yellow corn to the Piggly Wiggly. Mr. Smith looked at it and said, 'Buster (that was my Daddy's name) come over here and look at this.' He pointed at a couple of 3-peck baskets of old corn on the side of a shelf and said, 'Buster, this here yellow corn weren't any good. You are going to have to take it back.'

And my daddy asked him, 'How long has it been in the store, Mr. Smith?' And Mr. Smith said, 'It came in last week. It just weren't no good from the start.'

And my daddy knew he had him there. He said, 'Well, I guess I got you there, Mr. Smith. You see, we deliver white corn one week and yellow corn the next week. That there from last week is yellow corn and last week was a white corn week for us and so you must of got it from someone else.' Mr. Smith owned up that he could of made a mistake and didn't push it any further."

George paused. "After we got in the truck, my daddy said, 'I wish

I didn't have to deal with that cheatin' son of a bitch, but I guess I do. It's easy and he pays pretty good. We gotta make a livin' somehow.'"

George grinned. "One time we made a really good sale at the farmer's market. This doctor saw us driving up and bought the whole load of corn at retail and paid us extra to deliver it to his house. This made Daddy happy and he said he would buy me some new shoes. So we went to Kessler's and I told him that I would really like to have some basketball shoes so I could play basketball that winter. I knew I could make the school team, but I had to practice barefoot 'cause the coach wouldn't let me wear my brogans on the gym floor. Well, Daddy told me that I could only get one pair of shoes and if I wanted basketball shoes, that would be ok. So, I got some Converse All Stars. Black, with a white sole. High tops. Man, I was proud of those shoes. You know how your daddy or granddaddy had to 'walk ten miles through the snow to go to school?' Well, daddy only had to walk five miles to school – when he went – which wasn't often. Now me, I had it easy, I just had to walk two miles to the bus stop. But I did walk it barefoot. I always took my basketball shoes off and tied the laces together and hung them over my shoulder. I didn't want to wear them out on the gravel road."

George looked at Bud and asked, "What about you, Bud? I can tell by the way you do things that you're an old redneck." Bud had been in a halfway trance, listening, obviously going back to his own childhood. He looked up, stuck his hands in his pockets, and rocked back and forth on his heels and toes.

"Wa'al," he said, "there was eight of us children and Daddy made sure that we was in school every day the door was open. We only had a mule and buggy until we got a pickup when I was about twelve. I was third next to the youngest. We didn't go to church much 'cause it was right hard to get everybody ready and there with the wagon. But, I still remember my maw. She'd sit in her rocker every night that went by and make us all gather around her and she'd read us verse from the Bible. My youngest sister's still got that Bible. And that Bible has still got everybody's name in it.

"There sure is a lot of stuff kids today don't understand. Two of them things is working and Christmas. Me and my brothers and sisters would start picking cotton after school about three weeks before fall break. That way we had a head start on it when fall break came along. That two weeks of fall break, we were all in the cotton from dawn to dark. It'd break your back, but we kept at it because we knew that it had to be done for us to eat that winter. We'd get the wagon loaded. It took two mules and it was long with tandem wheels in the back. It had sides on it built what looked like up to the sky when I was a kid. Then, Friday night, we'd all climb up on the wagon and Daddy would drive it to town. We rode and spent the night on top of the cotton. You never seen a better bed. Man, it was soft, except some of the burrs and seeds got down in your coveralls sometimes. We'd get to the gin sometime late at night and sleep until about five in the morning when Daddy would get us up for breakfast. We had a bucket of fatback and biscuits that Maw had made for us. A lot of the kids from the other farms ate breakfast at the diner, but we had better things to do with our money.

"Daddy would make a deal with the foreman at the gin and he would stay with the wagon to make sure that everything got done right. He'd get a small advance on his money, though and he would give each of us fifteen cents to go to the movie and a dime to buy ice cream with. That movie was something else. It had news, something called coming attractions, cartoons, all kinds of other stuff and then cowboy movies with folks like Lash Larue, Gene Autry and Roy Rogers. Every once in a while we got a Hopalong Cassidy movie. I liked him.

"While we was at the movie, Momma and Daddy went shopping. They got bunches of stuff for the farm and lots of things like flour and sugar. We grew most all of the stuff we needed to eat. The last thing they would do was to get new coveralls and a new pair of brogans for each one of us kids. Momma would get a little cloth to make dresses for the sisters. I think she got a little red ribbon, too. That was put away and it was what we all got for Christmas. And Christmas was fun back then. We had lots of food and played with all the cousins, and it weren't all uptight like it is now. But, you know, them people in town, they did call us rednecks."

Harce added his part. "Yeah, they call us rednecks because they figured people from the country didn't know how to behave in town. I bet we behaved better than anybody else. When we used to take stuff to town, that's when I learned how to fight. I got to where I would fight some city kid who even looked at me wrong. The football coach wanted me to play football. I tried it out, but he told me I was too mean and all I was supposed to do was tackle the other guy, not get him down and hit on him. Hell, they didn't even think about running that football past me.

"But you know, we might of been rednecks, but we knew how to do stuff. We knew how to fix a truck that wouldn't run, and build houses and barns and ramjet pumps for water. My Grandma knew how to churn butter and sew clothes with a needle and thread. We knew how to butcher meat and how to hunt and how to grow our own food. Hell, Ol' Hank Jr. was right on the money when he sang that song *A Country Boy Can Survive*. We weren't afraid of work and we knew how to do stuff. Let them say what they want. All we ever needed from the store was sugar, flour, and ribbons for the girls. "

I paid attention and might have nudged the conversation toward the difference between rednecks and "white trash." Bud jumped all over that one and George Adams agreed.

Bud said, "A redneck might not have no money, but he does everything he can to get some. White trash don't never have no money and they don't seem to care."

George added, "White trash does better in town 'cause they can get on welfare and not think it is shameful."

Bud carried it on. "White trash is the people with the tumbling down house and dogs under the porch and pregnant daughters. Rednecks work, and they care about things and they know how to do things. That's the difference. White trash is really the ones they make the jokes about."

George told us, "I want you to look at what is important to rednecks. They love their trucks, they enjoy country music and that came down the line from church music. And then there's NASCAR, horse racing and chicken fights. That comes from who can come up with the best of everything and make it work for them. I think rednecks are the backbone of the United States. Tell me I'm wrong and you can kiss my ass."

I owned up that I would never complain about cold water again.

DRUGS IN THE COLONS

It was the fall of 1999, and everybody in The Colons was busy piling up firewood, butchering and processing hogs and cows and stockpiling gasoline and ammunition. Louann was busy salting down hams and hanging them in the newly-built smokehouse. Cases and cases of beer were hidden in the woods under armed guard. The word was out that a cataclysm was coming when the clock turned over to the new century. It was widely accepted that anything from civil war and strife to Armageddon was approaching. The residents of The Colons were going to be ready.

Harce had never "collected" from me for welding my greenhouse together, and it was payback time. I was in The Colons at his house. Harce had decided to build a small greenhouse for Louann and I was to supervise.

"Oh, well," I thought. "Payback is payback." I had bent the pipes for the arches and Harce had plenty of coat hangers on hand and he had recharged his torch.

Harce was building. He was in his element. He was a dynamo. "All right, John, you show Kickstand and Jeffrey where to weld the stringers. Me and you will lay out the tables down the sides and put the cages in.

I gave him a blank stare. "Cages?"

"Yeah. We're going to put the cages under the tables. We can use the cages to hold up the tables and then we don't have to put legs on them."

I repeated, "cages?" I paused. "I thought the greenhouse was so you could grow tomatoes and have them in case the grocery stores all got shut down January first."

Harce got impatient with me. He always thought that if something was worked out in his head, then everyone else should have the same thing worked out in their heads. Reading the inside of Harce's head was kind of scary to me.

"Yeah, John, don't you understand? Cages for the rabbits."

"Rabbits?" I asked.

"Man, John, I thought you was pretty smart. Listen to this, now. I ain't going to tell you but once. You gotta heat the tomato plants, right?"

"Right." I had absolutely no idea where this was going to go. "I thought you were going to use a wood heater."

I could see that I was about to try Harce's patience. He started talking and waving his hands around. "Don't you see? I built these rabbit cages. We use the cages to line the sides of the greenhouse and then we build the tables on top of them. You got to think about things and work them out, especially if our economy is going to crash in a month or two."

He pointed at the cages. "See, rabbits have this really hot body heat. They generate a bunch of heat 'cause they eat a bunch and they move around a bunch, and they work at breeding a bunch. The heat comes up under the plants and heats the roots and that makes the plants think the ground is warm like in summertime and they grow better."

He paused for all of that to sink in. I merely raised my eyebrows and gently shook my head. This kind of reasoning was beyond me.

"And then," he continued, "and then there's the rabbit crap. It's loaded with fertilizer and we mix it with the sawdust and leaves and other stuff and we get compost for our potting soil."

He stopped and grinned. I suggested that he had done a lot of thinking.

"And then," he continued, "and then we got lots and lots of meat to make Brunswick stew and you know how much everybody likes that. With all the restaurants and barbecue joints closed because of nobody having anything, I can corner the market on Brunswick stew."

I said the only thing I could think of. "Harce, that is totally amazing."

I worked with Kickstand and Jeffrey. They didn't need much instruction and they went about the job in a most professional manner, so I helped Harce with the cages. After a couple of hours, the amount of work that had been done was amazing. The welding was done, and Kickstand yelled, "Break time!" We all headed for the swings on the porch. Harce got a beer for me and two for himself. Kickstand and Jeffrey got out their material and started rolling a joint.

I made an observation. "That's some pretty slick welding."

Kickstand never raised his head, but spoke as he concentrated on rolling the joint. "Ought to be good welding. Ain't many people can get a couple of certified boilermakers to put a greenhouse together with coat hangers. Piece of cake."

I thought, "boilermaker?" I looked at Kickstand. "I thought a boilermaker was a drink with a shot glass of liquor dropped down in a mug of beer."

I wasn't being a smartass, that's actually what I thought. Kickstand paused long enough to lick the rolling paper and smooth out the joint. "Naw, that drink was named after boilermakers. That's their invention. Boilermakers are a different kind of people."

I observed his tattoos, his ponytail, his scruffy beard and the funny hat on his head and decided that he might be telling me the truth.

He continued, "Being a boilermaker is a different way of life. First, you have to go through a long process of training. You have to be an apprentice for a couple of years, then you get to be a journeyman, then, if you are really good, you can get to be a certified boilermaker."

"What does a boilermaker do?"

"There are ten boilermakers, five journeymen, and five apprentices on a crew. That's twenty men. When these big plants shut down for repairs or maintenance or new installations, one or more crews move in and make sure everything is in good working order and that new installations are perfect. We work with refrigeration and steam, so it takes a master welder to do the job and make sure it is done right. A lot of our work is done thirty or forty feet in the air. It is hotter'n hell in the summer and cold as a witch's tit in the winter. We got to get in, get the job done, and get out, because the plant is losing money while we are working."

He paused while they passed the joint around. I passed it up with my usual observation. "I don't do that. It gets in the way of my beer drinking."

"Boilermakers make pretty good money," Kickstand continued. "When we work, we work eighty hours a week or more. It really busts your butt, but the money is good. The only problem is, we will work on a job for a while and then when we finish we will get laid off and we live on unemployment. A good boilermaker will make over a thousand dollars a week when he's working, but he spends it like a rich kid in a candy shop. Then when there ain't no work for a while, there's nothing left." The joint came back around.

I pointed at the marijuana. "What about smoking dope? Don't they have drug tests if everything has to be so perfect?"

Kickstand exhaled a cloud of smoke, passed the joint to Harce, and resumed. He was enjoying his audience. "I'm telling you, man. We do hard work in uncomfortable places. All the welders I know smoke dope. This don't mean all of them smoke dope. I wouldn't go that far. I'm just saying that all the welders I know smoke dope. I know most of them. They have drug tests, but the thing is that if they run off all of the welders that smoke dope, they wouldn't have no welders. They know that. Every once in a while, it will come time for a drug test and the supervisor will come around and tell us, 'drug test tomorrow' and we will all go home and drink a quart of Quick Flush and that will wash all the stuff out of your system for 24 hours. Some of the guys buy clean pee from guys like you, John, who don't never smoke dope. They carry it in a Visine bottle under their arm so it will stay warm and they use it instead of their own. There's all kinds of tricks. There's a story that one guy got some from his wife and they called him in and told him he was pregnant. I don't know about that."

He continued. Talking about marijuana was fun. "And it ain't just boilermakers that smoke dope. There's doctors and lawyers and schoolteachers and all kinds of people who use it. It's going to change, though, 'cause they are getting new ways to test for drugs that will be hard to beat. I heard that there is one test coming that will analyze a piece of your hair. I don't know what's going to happen." He pointed at my beer can. "Most everybody gets high one way or the other some time in their life. They have different reasons. For me, it makes one of the nastiest jobs in the world bearable."

I asked, "Where does the marijuana come from?"

"Around here, a lot of it is home grown. This here we're smoking is some of Harce's home grown. Nobody knows where he grows it and he ain't going to tell, but it is some really good stuff. We ain't charging him money for today, he's paying us with home grown. Then there's big growers in Oregon that use the national forest land. I hear it is like a war zone up there. Over in Holland, Georgia, there's these really good dope growers. Their daddies were moonshiners, but when they legalized liquor sales in this part of the state back in the late sixties, the moonshiners like to of went out of business. Luckily for them, the hippies made marijuana popular and they switched from moonshine to dope. A lot of it comes in from Columbia and Mexico. There's a bunch of it around."

He paused, took a drag on the joint, blew out the smoke, sipped on his beer and continued, "You know, we talked about how much of it comes around one time. I wondered just exactly how many tons of marijuana get smoked in New York City in one day."

I was beginning to feel rather ignorant. "What about other drugs?" I asked. "I've heard about heroin, cocaine, and crack cocaine. What about those?"

"Well, everybody knows better than to shoot smack. That's what they call heroin. And cocaine, well, that's for rich people. I heard it's messed up a bunch of lawyers and such, but it's easier to ship and smuggle, and the smugglers are trying to get people to use coke instead of smoking dope, but smoking dope is pretty safe and it's good when you're working—or relaxing."

"Crack cocaine is for stupid people. I talked to one guy who was addicted bad to crack cocaine. He told me that the first time you do crack cocaine, you are addicted. You'll never get over trying to find that first high. I've seen a bunch of people messed up on crack cocaine and I wouldn't touch it with a ten foot pole. Actually, I just like smoking dope and drinking beer and I think that's what I'll stay with. I'm doing good and I don't want to take no chances."

It was about time to go back to work, but Kickstand added one more piece of information about drugs. At the time, I found it interesting. Years later, along with many other people, I found it horrifying.

Kickstand said, "I hear that there's something new coming down from the moonshine hills in Tennessee. They say you can take a hit off of it and work all day. They say you can use this stuff and get more done than any four men. And, they say it is easy to manufacture, so it is easy to get and easy to distribute. I don't know about all of that. I'll wait and see. I hear it's kind of like the old diet pills, only multiply it by a hundred."

I said, "Kickstand, you seem to really know a lot. What do they call this new drug?"

He looked at me like I was stupid. "You ain't heard about it?"

He paused. "They call it methamphetamine."

He paused. "Meth, for short. Let's go back to work."

We finished the greenhouse. I was too tired for a story at the end of the day, so I just went home and took a nap. I later wished that I had paid more attention to Kickstand.

chapter 13
DUI

On a Sunday morning a week or so later, Ponytail drove up to the house at about 7:30. I was still drinking my coffee.

"Hey, Ponytail, what's up?"

"H-h-h Harce wants you to get him out of jail."

Harce had been in jail several times, mostly for getting in fights, so I was not really surprised.

"What's he in there for?"

Ponytail was getting back in the truck to leave. He never hung around for long. "Hhhhe got b-b-b-b-bbusted for d-d-d-ddrinking and d-d-d-ddriving last nnnnight." He drove off.

I had been here before. Getting someone out of jail wasn't a hard thing to do, it was just time consuming and a lot of trouble. It was also expensive. I called the jail.

"You got Harce in there?" I didn't have to use Harce's last name, they knew him at the jail.

"Yup. DUI."

"How much is the bond?" I asked.

"Twelve hundred fifty dollars," came the reply.

"I'll be there in a little while," I responded, looking up the number for Coleman Bail Bonding. I found the number, called, and made an appointment for a representative from the bonding company to meet me at the jail in an hour. I woke Marsha up, helped her feed the dogs and cats, listened to her complain and complain and complain, and we got in the truck to go get our friend.

When rich folks go to jail for DUI, somebody merely goes in and puts up a property bond. This is to guarantee that the offending culprit will show up for court on the given date. When a redneck goes to jail, on the other hand, they need someone to call the bail bondsman. The bail bonding company holds a state license and has shown sufficient asset—mostly real estate—to cover many bonds. They send a representative who checks out the character and "flight risk" of the offender balanced against the severity of the charge. They have the power to decide whether or not they consider the culprit a safe risk and if they choose, they will sign the bond and charge a ten percent fee for their services. If the "bondee" doesn't show up for court, the bonding company must find them or pay the entire bail amount. Bail bondsmen are generally not really nice people – it goes with the job – but I had done a good bit of business with Mr. Coleman and he knew me and, of course, he knew Harce.

I walked into the jail lobby, took a seat in one of the recycled kindergarten school desks that didn't have room for my long legs and waited for Mr. Coleman to show up. After a little while, I heard some grunting and smiled as I pictured the greatly overweight bondsman squeezing through the doorway. I didn't have to turn and look; I had watched him before. He walked up to me with his briefcase. "Good to see you again, John. Here, fill out these papers."

I tried unsuccessfully to avoid looking at him as I took the papers. He was a big man with a ponderous gut hanging over his belt. His shirt had once been white but it was now multicolored with coffee stains, a large spot of tomato soup, some chocolate where he had wiped his hands, and a grey strip at the top of the collar. There were ovals of skin showing through between the buttons over his stomach where the fabric had been pulled too tight. Folds of his chin hung over the grey shirt collar.

I took the papers and concentrated on filling them out. When I finished, Mr. Coleman carefully studied all of the entries, nodded his head, got out his receipt book and held out his hand for money.

I counted out one hundred and twenty five dollars in cash.

"They've added on a fifteen dollar processing fee," he said. I pulled my last twenty out of my pocket and handed it to him. He made change and gave me a receipt and walked to the jail receptionist window. "Let's get Harce out of here," he told the clerk. More papers were signed. The clerk disappeared.

"There you go," said Mr. Coleman. "Good seeing you again, John. I always appreciate a good repeat customer."

I waited and waited. I knew that Marsha was very unhappy waiting in the truck and that I would hear about it later. After a while, I heard a couple of voices in the back of the jail yelling something like, "See you Harce" and "Keep it in the road, Harce." I grinned because I was sure that Harce had visited at least several of his many good friends. Then the massive steel door opened and Harce walked out carrying a plastic bag which contained his belt, his shoelaces, and his wallet. He had a grin on his face and a look in his eyes that showed that he could think of better places to be. We got out of there. It was time to deliver Harce to The Colons. He wasn't in much of a mood to talk and the trip was rather quiet. We stopped by the bootlegger's house on the way and got a six pack which we split. Harce turned up a beer and that seemed to loosen him up and he told us about his experience.

"I knew I was pushing the limit, but I was on my way home and I didn't want to call somebody to come get me so I turned on the road to The Colons and I knew I was all right when I made it over the one-lane bridge and I don't know what them po-lice was doing up there but they got behind me and I knew I was in trouble. They was following close and I figured they was after me so I took out my bag of marijuana and stuffed it down through the rusted out hole in the floorboard of the truck and I sure did hate that. Then the blue lights came on and that was when I decided that I didn't want my truck towed so I just kind of kept driving – slow, kind of like O.J. did – and they followed me with the lights flashing and then right before I got to my driveway, the siren came on and I stopped up there by the fence and got out of the truck. The po-lice jumped out of their car and pulled out their guns and I held my hands up in the air and Rocky and

Marvin came running out here barking and the po-lice said, 'call off them dogs' and Louann come running out of the house and started yelling and they pushed me down on the hood of the car and the po-lice said 'get down on the car' and then he said, 'call off them dogs' and when I straightened up and tried to call off the dogs, he said, 'get down on the car' and then it happened all over again and I told him we needed to lighten up a bit. And then Louann got the dogs. They made me blow in this thing and one of them said, 'point one oh, borderline.' And the other one said, 'but he was eluding and he didn't stop' and so they arrested me. I was happy, though, because they didn't beat me up or nothing."

Harce got quiet again as we pulled into his driveway.

I checked out the progress that Harce had made on building his monstrous gazebo while he went and dug through his firewood pile to find his coffee can with his money in it so he could pay me back for my bonding agent expenditures. I could tell he was grateful, too, because he paid for the beer and didn't charge me for my three cans. Louann was all concerned that he was alright and called him "poor baby." Marsha didn't say much of anything until she and I were on the way home and that's when she cut loose on how much she liked to sleep late on Sunday morning and how it was lunchtime and her day was ruined. She didn't stop until we got home. I lost count of how many times she said the same thing. It was a lot, though. But I really didn't blame her. My morning had been ruined, also. Harce owed me big time.

A couple of weeks later, I called my friend Jim who was a pretty good lawyer. He went to the judge with Harce and they negotiated a *nolo contendere* plea and Harce had to pay a nine hundred dollar fine and be on probation for a year. This meant that he had to check in with a probation officer once a week and pay a thirty dollar a week fee. The regulations in Georgia stated that he had to go to "Driving School" which was commonly called "DUI School" in order to get his license back. Harce's observation was, "They done made a believer out of me. I won't never drink and drive again." He never did, either, as far as I know. Ponytail was happy. This created a lot of extra income for him.

All of this was a financial disaster for someone of Harce's means. He had to come up with a lot of money. I guess it was a good thing, though, because one of my customers needed a special, 18- foot curved Japanese bridge. I was able to watch Harce do a special piece of work.

Harce went to the site and measured and studied the project. He made a list of materials and bought a pick-up load of treated one-by-fours and several gallons of glue. He worked all one night building a twenty-foot work table from sawmill wood in his barn. Next, he measured carefully and placed a series of dowels in a gentle double curve down the length of the table.

He brought in a Coleman gas stove and a pressure cooker. He glued together two ten foot pieces of four-inch schedule eighty pvc pipe with a solid cap on one end. He modified the cap for the other end so that it screwed on and he installed a gas fitting in the middle of it. He built a twenty foot level trough outside next to the barn, lined it with a solid sheet of black plastic, and filled it with water. Then, he placed the treated one by fours in the water, carefully, so as not to poke a hole in the plastic, set some concrete blocks on top of the lumber, drank a beer, and went to bed. He had been working non stop for two solid days and nights. He was ready to go. I wondered where anyone could get so much energy. It took a long time to find out.

Starting the next day, Harce examined the treated one-by-fours every day for a couple of days before he declared them ready. He filled the pressure cooker with water and turned on the heat. He placed three of the one by fours in the pvc pipe, screwed the cap on and hooked up a copper pipe from the relief valve on the pressure cooker to the gas fitting on the pipe. "The top must be screwed on just right," he observed. "If you get it too loose, you lose all your steam, and if you get it too tight, it will blow up on you. Actually, I need a pressure gauge, but I ain't got enough money, so I'll have to do it by feel." He carefully watched the process as the steam from the pressure cooker filled up the pipe. Periodically, he would loosen or tighten the cap on the end of the pipe. He was oblivious to anything going on around him and was lost in total concentration.

After about an hour, Harce got a smile on his face and said, "Just right." He turned off the pressure cooker, put on his welder's gloves, removed the cap from the pipe and extracted the pieces of wood. They were very limber. He ran his hands lovingly over the wood. "You know," he observed, "if you get the wood just right you can tie a knot in it." He carefully took each piece of wood to the table with the dowels and worked it into the double "s" curve, clamping it tightly. "Next," he said, "we will heat up some more wood and put layers in the frame. A double layer of glue goes between each layer and we end up with a laminated beam. When everything dries out and cures, the curves will be locked in and will stay that way forever." He picked up some more wet one-by-fours and started the steaming process anew.

The process took a week. He made three laminated runners for the bridge itself, and then he made two laminated hand rails with a matching curve. He sculpted all edges with a router and sanded it for hours and hours. The project became a masterpiece of prefabrication. When he got all of the parts to the job site, everything fit to perfection. There were no nails or screws. Holes had been drilled in just the right places and the entire project was put together with wooden pegs and glue. I was totally impressed. And, you know, I had never seen anyone who loved a piece of wood quite like Harce did. The delighted customer gave Harce his check and we went directly to the bank where he cashed it. "I never did believe in checking accounts," he observed. "I like to have cash in my hands. That makes money real."

We eventually got back to Harce's house where he walked triumphantly into the kitchen, pulled the wad of money out of his pocket, slid a chair up to the kitchen table, and started counting out piles of bills.

"For the lawyer....

"For the fine....

"Two hundred ten damn dollars for DUI school....

"Two hundred fifty damn dollars to take to Dalton for license reinstatement....

"Money for probation fees....

"Money so Ponytail can drive me to school and to Dalton....

"Good. I sure do hate owing money to anybody....

"I reckon that about does it and there's enough for me and you to get some beer, John."

So we did.

chapter 14
A LEG AND A STORY

Harce had been working on his gazebo longer than I had known him. I had been amazed from the first time I saw it, not only because of the quality of the work, but because of its overall size. This gazebo was huge. It wasn't too large, mind you. If it had been excessively large, the size would have taken away from the intimacy provided by a gazebo. I did think, however, that if he had extended the floor by another two thirds of an inch, it would have gone past these limits.

The gazebo was finally finished. Harce was proud of it. He had invited Kickstand, Ponytail, and me to "christen the gazebo like they do a boat, only we're going to use bottles of beer instead of bottles of champagne and we're going to drink the beer instead of throwing the bottles up against the gazebo. That will be more fun and it won't scratch the wood. Anybody scratches the wood on this here gazebo is in for me opening up a whole barrel of whupass and spreading it all over them. I guarantee it."

Harce had made it clear that my invitation included my bringing the beer. That was all right with me and I invested wisely in the second best beer in the whole world: bottled Rolling Rock in the green bottles from Latrobe, Pennsylvania. I guess the only better malt beverage ever made was Red Cap Ale, but I hadn't seen any of that in years. I also picked up the ingredients for Ponytail's favorite mixed drink which he called a "Sonic." This was half and half tonic water and club soda with a twist of lime. Ponytail didn't drink alcohol or smoke marijuana. He didn't need to for two reasons. First, he called himself a professional driver and he therefore couldn't drink, and second, Ponytail had spent his entire life in outer space without ever needing any outside help.

Marsha had driven us to The Colons for the gathering. She and Louann felt more comfortable having their own conversation inside the house. This was all right with Harce. He wanted to drink beer, show off his gazebo, and tell stories. I knew how to get the party started. I passed out some beer, watched Kickstand start rolling a joint for him and Harce, and I said, "Well, Harce, what kind of wood is that?"

Harce grinned and jumped up. "Did you see the cedar shingles? I split them myself. You see, you take a piece of cedar wood that is just right and you take this thing called a froe and a mallet and you split them shakes off of that piece of wood. Them shingles take anything, and the way you put them on, they won't leak ever. If you do it right. And these here six-by-six uprights are solid red oak. I ran a router over the corners with a Roman Ogee bit and cut that kind of rounded edge. Then I hand sanded them with six different grades of sandpaper, from 80 grit to 600 grit emery paper. I think that grit thing means the number of grits – not the kind you eat, the kind you put on sandpaper – per inch. I don't know, something like that, anyway, the higher the grit, the smoother the sandpaper. And that ain't shellac on them, neither, that's fifteen coats of rubbed on linseed oil and it is buffed with carnuba wax."

"The four-by-six roof joists are made of heart pine. You won't find nothing like that in no lumber yard. The floor is tongue and grooved white oak. That's about the best flooring you can get. These boards are eight inches wide. You can't buy that nowhere, neither. I did the tongue and groove with a special router bit that I mounted on my work bench so it wouldn't mess up. The floor is made out of the centers of three trees. You see them three stumps over there by the barn? That's where I started. He threw his beer bottle in a barrel. This here's pretty good for yankee beer, John, give me another one."

I handed him a beer. Harce caught his breath, twisted off the top, took a swig and cranked right back up. "Now this railing here," he rubbed it lovingly, slowly, and sensuously, actually smiling at the wood, "This railing here is made of carefully selected poplar. You see how you don't hardly notice much grain in it? If you look a little closer, you'll see that the ends of the grain match perfectly where the wood is joined. Now, you might think that is an accident, and it might be an accident, but it ain't. I spent three months on this handrail, started with a draw knife and ended up with 600 grit emery paper. I turned the balusters on Grandpaw's homemade lathe. They're made out of cypress from Louisiana. Friend of mine brought me the cypress."

Last, and definitely not least, he pointed to the ornate gingerbread cornice pieces on each side of the uprights. "You ever heard of the Royal Pawlonia tree?" he asked. "There used to be a bunch of them around here until some Japanese guy came and started buying them all up. I did some sawmilling for him. It turned out that Pawlonia is the most expensive wood per board foot in the world. It makes veneer better than any other. There ain't much around here no more. I heard old Jack Dickey is growing a plantation of Pawlonia down in South America somewhere. He gave me one of his business cards and it was printed on Pawlonia wood. Looked just like cardboard til you studied it. Anyway, I happened to forget to give some of that wood to the Japanese guy and that's what I made the cornices out of. I sawed it one quarter inch thick and I cut the designs out of it with a hand coping saw. I used the smallest, finest blades I could get. Used over forty of them. Give me another one of them beers, John."

Harce sat down, kind of out of breath. He hadn't told us yet about the notched and pegged benches built into the railings, or about the obviously handmade blades on the ceiling fan. I was afraid to ask. We all sat there for a moment, all mellowed out and I decided that it was time to ask another question that I had been afraid to ask for some time. It was a personal question and personal questions were generally not allowed in the redneck society.

Kickstand passed a joint to Harce. He took a big hit on it and I asked, "Harce, tell me about what's wrong with your leg?"

Harce choked on the smoke and coughed loudly. "What the hell are you talking about?" he asked, unconsciously reaching down and gently rubbing his right shin.

I didn't back down. "Well, you limp on it, you never wear shorts, it seems swollen or something all the time, and every time you sit down, you rub it like you are doing right now."

"I had a motorcycle accident," he said quietly.

Kickstand looked up. "He thought he was Evil Kneivel only, Evil generally stayed sober when he rode."

Harce continued, "I thought I'd go ride over that ridge over there on Jeffrey's new dirt bike. I went over the ridge at 60 and left the ground and all I remember is when I woke up, I was on the porch and I had this big gash on my shin from my knee to my ankle."

Kickstand looked up. "There weren't nobody here sober enough to drive and we didn't have no phone to call no ambulance and Harce couldn't afford one, noway. Louann treated it."

Harce was sitting there with his elbows on his knees staring at the floor. He shook his head slowly back and forth. "I had insurance with the company I was welding for, but I lost it when I got laid off because they lost their contract. I wanted to get some more, but I couldn't afford it, being laid off like that, and then after I hurt my leg, I couldn't get it covered, noway. Now, if I go to the doctor about it, I can't pay for it and I'm scared they will take my house or my land or my sawmill. I just don't have any idea what to do about it. It's been like this for a long time and me and Louann keep it clean. It don't seem to get infected, but it don't never get no better, neither. I worry about it all the time." Harce was lost in thought. He looked me square in the eye. "You got any idea what for me to do, John?"

I matched his stare. "Give me a few days to work on it, maybe I know someone who can help."

And that was all of the talking that was going to be done about the leg. I had just seen a side of Harce that very few people knew existed. In a little while, Harce looked up and said, "Hey, John, tell us a story. Tell us a story about jail."

"I don't know a good story about jail," I replied. I thought for a minute. "I know a story Grover Higgins told me one time about being a prisoner of war. Will that do?"

"You talking about Grover Higgins the surveyor? I liked him.

He was a good guy."

"Yeah," I replied. "Grover told me about being in the German prisoner of war camp with a bunch of Alabama and Georgia boys." I really wasn't in a storytelling mood, so I tried to get out of it as quickly as I could. "Grover told me that they had to work on the roads and it was pretty hard work. He said they worked all day while this guard with a shotgun sat on this wagon and watched them all day while his German Shepherd sat there next to him. He said they had plenty to eat but it was always potato soup and cabbage. They never got any meat.

"There was always a group of German soldiers with rifles standing around behind the boss' wagon and there was no way they could escape. They were chained. The prisoners were fed at sunup in the mornings, worked all day, and then got fed again at night. Always potato soup and cabbage. The German foreman liked them because they were good redneck boys and they knew how to get the job done. Grover said it was about the end of the war right before they got liberated by the Allied troops. He said everybody was surprised one night when they all had meat in their potato soup."

I paused for effect.

"The next day, the German foreman was all upset. His dog was missing."

Kickstand laughed. "They ate the damn dog, didn't they?"

Harce asked, "Is that the whole story? You're slipping, John."

"Hell, Harce." I shrugged my shoulders, palms in the air. "I don't know any jail stories. How about Kickstand? I bet he knows one."

Harce kind of grinned. "Tell him, Kickstand. Tell him how that guard in Reidsville kept you from being a murderer."

We opened up fresh Rolling Rocks while Kickstand rolled a fresh joint and lit it. They never passed the joints to me any more because they knew I would say the same thing—"It gets in the way of my beer drinking."

Kickstand leaned way back against the poplar railing, took a healthy swig of beer and started. "I guess it was about six years ago my old lady kicked me out of the house. Maybe it was seven, I don't know. Something like that. Anyway, I was in between boilermaker jobs at the time and I didn't have nowhere to go stay and so I made a deal with my Grandma that I could stay at her house if I was neat and clean and split the firewood and helped her with the cows and the garden. Grandpa had died a couple of years before and he had always made 'shine and he farmed and done right good.

"Well, me and Grandma did pretty good together. I always was a worker and she liked that and since I had grown up on the farm, I knew how to do everything just like she wanted. She didn't much seem to want me to bring girls around but after that last woman, that was ok with me. And Grandma didn't much mind if my buddies from work hung around and drank beer. She kind of liked the company and she would laugh and joke with them. Sometimes we would go out behind the house by the garden and smoke some weed. We hid it from her at first, but when she found out she didn't much seem to care. She said smoking weed and drinking shine like Grandpa did was kind of the same thing. Hell, she even tried it a couple of times.

"Grandma fixed me up a bedroom and I got a tv and as long as I kept the door closed it was all right if I sat around in my shorts and watched the ball game and drank beer and burped. She didn't care. It's funny, too, because that was why I got kicked out of the other house. Oh, well.

"Anyway, back to the marijuana. See, while we were smoking out by the garden, there were a few pot plants that came up in the tomato patch. One day, Grandma showed me one of the plants and asked me if it was a weed. I told her some people called it that. I also told her that it was against the law for her to grow it and that she shouldn't leave it in the garden. Then she asked me how much it sold for and I showed her a forty dollar bag. She owned up to how that was more than shine cost and easier to move around. That was it. She never brought it up again and the plants weren't in her garden no more and I forgot about the conversation. And it was a while before I noticed that some back issues of my *High Times* magazine were missing. In case you don't know, that's a magazine that's mostly about marijuana.

"I went back to work for a while and like I told you, boilermakers put in a lot of hours and you're tired big time when you get home at night and I didn't pay much attention to Grandma other than feeding the cows and hauling in the firewood. We had plenty of firewood because I had cut and split a whole bunch when I was laid off. I didn't even think nothing of it when Grandma got me up one Sunday morning and told me she wanted me to put this great big padlock on the attic door. I just got my tools and put it on there. I worked pretty hard and pretty long hours for about six months and never thought about that padlock. Grandma was by herself most of the time. And, Jimmy, down the road, after I had been working about three weeks, he asked me about all them UPS trucks, and I told him I didn't know nothing about no UPS trucks and later he told me they had stopped coming. I didn't think nothing about that, neither.

"Then I got laid off again and I was hanging around the house and Grandma one day said, "Come here, Sonny Boy, I want to show you something." Well, we went up the stairs to the attic and she opened the padlock and she opened the door and you could have knocked me down with a boiled possum tail. I never seen anything like it. There was these big lights on tracks like they traveled back and forth and there was these big troughs and there was marijuana plants halfway up to the ceiling and they were pruned to perfection."

Kickstand looked at the floor and shook his head. "I never seen nothing like it." He paused. "Not to this day." He paused again. "I never seen nothing like it." Kickstand sat there for a while, just shaking his head. He took a sip of beer.

"Well, Grandma picked up a garbage bag and handed it to me. She said she had saved it for me when she pruned the plants. It was full of buds that she had cut off of the plants. That's the part you want. That's the good stuff. Grandma asked me if that was a hundred dollar's worth and I told her it was more like five hundred dollar's worth. She like to had a cow. She said there was a bunch more." He gazed at the floor again. "That was just the start.

"Well, she asked me if we could sell it like her and Grandpa sold their moonshine and I told her I knew a guy up in Chattanooga who would take all she could send and give us a bunch of money and he would ship it to New York."

Kickstand looked up at me. "You ever wonder how many

pounds of pot A DAY get smoked up there in New York?" He took a sip of beer. He stopped to silently roll another joint, lit it, and passed it to Harce. "Anyway, me and Grandma talked about it and we decided that we couldn't take it to Chattanooga in garbage bags and I told her about how it comes from Mexico in bales. She thought about it over night and the next morning she gave me some money to go to the Lowe's store and buy a garbage compactor. I did that and we put the garbage bags in it and we made that stuff up in bales. We made up ten of them. That's when I found out how smart Grandma was.

"Grandma said, 'Sonny boy,' (She always called me 'Sonny boy.') She said 'come over here and let me cut your ponytail off.' I didn't want my ponytail cut off but I knew better than to talk back to Grandma and so I let her do it. When she got through she made me go shave off my beard and I looked just like a banker from First Federal. And then she made me memorize some Bible verses. Like I said. I knew better than to argue with Grandma.

"Then, the next day, she took me out back and showed me an almost new Chevy conversion van that looked really nice. It was carpeted and had those double doors in the back that open out and have a spare tire on the back. I was impressed. She told me she rented it from the camper place down on the Alabama Road. It was pretty and I always liked a Chevy anyway. I told her I would be sure to keep the carpet and the leather seats clean. And then we loaded the packed garbage bags from the trash compactor in the back of the van and she took me in the house and she had a brand new black suit and a white shirt and a red tie for me to put on. She put a wore out Bible on the console next to the driver's seat and told me to go to see my friend in Chattanooga. She told me to go exactly two miles over the speed limit and if I got stopped, to use the Bible verses she had taught me and act like a preacher.

"Man, Grandma was smart. It worked just right. If I got into a license check or something, I would ask the cop if he had been saved and he would fidget and I would tell him he needed to get bathed in the blood of the lamb and he would glance at my license and insurance paper and get my ass right out of there. It went on for a while and everything would have been all right except I got stupid.

"You see, Grandma told me to be really careful, but that weed was really good and I got to liking it. It got to where it was boring driving to Chattanooga all the time and so I started keeping a little loose stuff under the carpet which was under the trash bag bales. Sometimes I would stop and go to the back and get a little out and smoke it. That's what happened. One time I guess I was kind of stoned and I didn't shut the back doors right. I was taking off from a stoplight downtown and the doors opened and one of them square bales of dope fell out."

He paused. He drained the Rolling Rock bottle. He looked out into the distance.

"It fell out right on the hood of the car behind me."

He paused. "It was a police car."

He paused. "The police honked his horn to tell me I had dropped something out of the back of the van.

The policeman got out and said, 'Hey, preacher, you dropped a box of Bibles or something.'

"I stared at him. He smelled it. I went to jail."

Kickstand stopped. He had drunk a lot of beer and smoked a lot of pot while telling the story. He leaned his head back on the railing and passed out.

I looked at Harce. "What the hell is this? That was not a jail story."

Harce laughed. "He ain't got to that part, yet."

I asked, "What about the part about the guard keeping him from being a murderer?"

Harce laughed. "He ain't got to that part yet, neither." He paused. "That's the good part."

"Please, please tell me what happened. What happened to his Grandma?" I was almost begging.

Harce laughed. "Cain't nobody tell that stuff like Kickstand. He passes out at the same place every time. You'll have to get him to finish it some other time. He's gone. Next time you see him, just look at him and say them last three words, 'I went to jail' and he'll start back up."

Well, there was nothing else to do.

And the beer was all gone, anyway.

I got Marsha and we went home.
My head was full of Rolling Rock.
And Kickstand's Grandma.
And Harce's leg.

chapter 15

VOCATIONAL REHABILITATION

A week or so later, I was doing a Japanese garden in the back yard of a friend in town. I knew J.T. worked for the state, helping people with handicaps. I told J.T. about Harce's leg and he told me about VR (Vocational Rehabilitation).

He said, "Have Harce contact Miss Lucy Wong at VR and she will get him to a doctor."

Harce got his appointment with Miss Wong, and Ponytail drove him to Rome at the appointed time.

The interview started with Miss Wong explaining, "VR is a work program. You do want to go to work, don't you?"

Harce replied, "I have a saw mill, but I don't work."

To which Miss Wong said, "But you do run the saw mill as your primary source of income, correct?"

Harce said, "I cut wood, then trade or sell it. It gets me by."

Miss Wong continued, "VR helps people with disabilities obtain, maintain or re-train for work. We'll say we are going to help you maintain your job running your saw mill."

Harce replied, "Whatever."

Miss Wong then took a look at Harce's leg, picked up the phone and made him an appointment with a doctor for the following week.

Harce got real nervous and said, "I ain't got no money to pay a Doc!"

Miss Wong said, "Don't worry, it won't cost you a thing. This is your tax dollars at work for you."

Harce looked at her rather suspiciously and said, "I ain't never paid no taxes, sept' on my beer at the store."

Miss Wong suppressed a laugh and said, "Whatever."

chapter 16
THE DRAGON

I really don't know why, but I had started drinking bloody Marys for breakfast. To begin, I would make a pot of coffee, drink a couple of cups, and then make a pitcher of bloody Marys and start putting them down. I was entering the third stage of alcoholism. I didn't know that then, but I do now. After a while, I did away with the coffee and just drank the bloody Marys

My day was made by:

Getting a buzz on.

Doing some work and drinking some beer.

Taking a nap.

Doing some work and getting a buzz on.

And there was a steady pain in the lower right side of my abdomen. I didn't know what that meant.

I had been slowly killing myself and was now accelerating the process. I don't think I had a suicide wish. I don't think I had any wishes at all. I had gone to The Valley, and there seemed to be no way for me to climb out.

Judge Hamilton once said of another friend, "John, if a man digs himself into a hole and needs to get out, help him. If you don't feel like helping him, at least don't throw dirt in on top of him." I had shunned all help. Either I didn't know I needed help or I didn't want help.

I don't know where my reason had located itself. Perhaps it was off in a cloud somewhere. I don't know, but it surely wasn't in a place that I was familiar with. One by one, I let down the people who depended on me. No one threw dirt down in the hole on me. I pulled it in on myself. I dug the hole deeper and deeper

Most days around that time, Harce would come to see me early in the morning. He got Ponytail to drive him to the house. Ponytail would go fishing while Harce and I talked or worked. Harce wasn't driving then because the police had put the fear of God in him. He knew he was going to drink, and he didn't want to get arrested again. His leg was refusing to heal. He was drinking a lot, also, and he needed some company so he showed up early enough that we could talk without being bothered.

He looked at me. "John, I don't know what is going to happen to my leg. The doctor said it needs to come off and I got scared and threw a fit and started throwing things and they threw my ass out of the office."

"They didn't call the cops?"

"Naw, they told me not to come back until I figured out how to act right."

"What did you do then?"

"I went and got some white likker and got drunk."

"I bet that helped a lot."

"Naw, I got even more scared and then I started seeing things and then I passed out."

"How's your leg today?"

He pulled up his pants leg and showed me a wrapping with a blood stain in the middle of it. He unwrapped the bandage and I looked at his leg. It just wouldn't heal. It had been like that for six months. Harce kept it really clean and washed it out all the time with peroxide and other things and miraculously, it hadn't gotten infected. I looked at his leg and looked back up at him.

"It doesn't seem to be getting worse, but it's not any better, either. I never saw anything like that. It just won't heal."

He looked down at the wound. "Barney told me—You know Barney, he was in the rice paddies in Nam—he said that they let flies lay eggs in a wound and the larvae would eat out the dead meat. The doctor told me that was correct. I just can't stand the thought of it. But, man, they want to cut off my damn leg. Can you imagine what that would be like? They want to cut it here." He pointed to a place right below his knee.

We stopped talking while I mixed a couple of drinks.

I took a sip, smacked my lips, and added a touch more of Tabasco.

"Don't you think that you would be somehow better off with something better or different below your knee?"

"Damn it, John, I thought you were my friend. I didn't know you would side with them damn doctors. They got to be able to do something."

Harce walked out, slamming the door, went and kicked Ponytail's truck tire, rammed his fist into the front fender and settled down a bit before returning and resuming the conversation. "I ain't never been scared of nothing. Not nothing. Not in my life."

He started rewrapping his bandage. "But this. But this is different."

Harce finished his bloody Mary, walked to the kitchen sink and rinsed out the glass, set it down and reached in the refrigerator for a beer. He popped the top and turned it up. "And now they tell me I got to stop drinking and smoking for a month before they can do anything. I don't know if I can do that."

I said, "Harce, you can do anything you want to do. You know that."

He thought about it for a moment. "AND WHAT IF I DON'T DAMN WANT TO?"

I looked away from his leg. My eyes accidentally stopped and stared into the deep vivid blue of his. "I think, Harce, that your choice is to quit drinking or die."

Harce was livid. "HEY, ASSHOLE, DON'T YOU THINK YOU'VE GOT THE SAME DAMN CHOICE? I'LL BET YOU CAN'T QUIT EITHER!"

There was silence. We stared at each other.

We stared for quite some time. It was one of those situations where the first one to speak loses.

"Well," we both finally said at the same time. Harce looked at me and grinned. "You think you can quit drinking?"

"Sure." I took a sip of my bloody Mary. "I could quit if I wanted to."

"You want to bet?"

"Yeah, I'll bet. But it's got to be a damn big bet. Big enough to make me want to quit."

He thought about it. "What do you want to bet? A hundred dollars?"

I laughed. "No, Harce. A hundred dollars ain't enough. How about if we bet your leg?"

"You mean if you quit drinking, let's say for a month, I got to give you my leg?"

I nodded. "Yeah, I'm tired of looking at it and hearing you bitch and moan about it."

Harce gave me a really funny look. "What do I get if I win?"

I laughed out loud. "You get to keep that nasty-ass leg, and die. Or else you get a new fake leg and live. I don't know what you get if you win. Which alternative is better?"

He thought about it. "But, if I have to pay up, I got to quit drinking for a month too. And I got to get my leg cut off."

I smiled. He got the point. I said, "How else are you going to be able to tell if I keep my part of the bargain? If you ain't drinking, you can smell beer on me. And, how else are you going to pay up?" I shook my finger in his face. "I don't ever lose a bet."

And that's how I quit drinking.

And that's how Harce ended up with a fake leg.

That was Thanksgiving, 2001.

Looking back, though, I wish I had known more about what was going on in The Colons

And I wish I had known more about depression.

And I will never be able to thank him enough for helping me to change my life.

Harce looked at me long and hard. "Are you really going to quit drinking?"

"I said I would. I shook on it. Anyway, after what you said to me, I guess it's about time." I thought a moment. "My friend Steve once said, 'I don't guess I ever knew anyone who screwed up by quitting drinking.'"

Harce thought that was pretty funny. He kind of giggled and said, "My grandpa and all of his friends always held that a man's word is his bond. Grandpa always said that this was the difference between a good, honest redneck and white trash."

I thought about that. "What about that rich lawyer I worked for who didn't pay me like he said he would?"

Harce laughed. "You needed to know my grandmaw. She always said, 'there's class and there's trash and no amount of money will make a difference between the two.' I guess that tells you where the rich lawyer stands, at least the way she would look at it." Harce thought about it. He obviously wanted to craft a well-thought-out verbal contract on our deal about drinking and his leg. "Now, we're both agreeing to quit drinking for at least thirty days, right?"

"Right."

"And I got to get my leg worked on. Right?"

"Right."

"And what about drinking after they fix my leg? Will you stay quit?"

I had to think long and hard. "I don't know, Harce."

He laughed. "Now, I guess that's an honest answer. Ok. You've got all I know about contracts. What do you know? Do you want to put it in writing?"

I said, "I'll tell you what my Uncle John told me about contracts and we'll go from there. Uncle John told me, 'son, there's two kinds of contracts. There's a long contract and a short contract. Of the two, the short contract is more binding.'"

Harce had to think about this. "That's pretty interesting. In other words, the short contract contains a promise of honor and fair dealing."

"That's the way I read it," I replied.

"And," he asked, "how short can a contract be?"

I knew the answer. "Uncle John said, 'there are two kinds of short contract: a written short contract and a verbal short contract. Of the two, the verbal contract is more binding.'"

Harce really liked this one. "All right," he said. "Then my Grandpa's people had the contract thing right to start with. If you said you were going to do something, you did it."

I asked, "And what did your Grandpa's people do if someone didn't keep the contract? Did they go to court or something?"

"Naw," he said. "They didn't want no truck with no courts. They kind of had a way of taking care of things all by themselves." He paused. "My grandpa would give someone the shirt off his back, but didn't nobody want to cross him."

We shook hands again. Harce asked, "Then we got a deal?"

"We got a deal. When do we start? Tomorrow?"

"Hell, no." He poured out his drink. "We go'n start right by God now."

I poured out my drink. Harce called Ponytail and left. I wouldn't see him again for two weeks.

I sat in the rocking chair on the porch and stared at the lake. I stared at it for a long, long time. I watched the cattails blowing in the wind and paid attention to the ripples as the wind moved them first one direction, then another. I listened to the birds. I paid close attention to the cardinals as I watched the females sit in the maple tree while the male ate his fill from the bird feeder. I watched as the male cardinal then moved to the tree and guarded the females as they ate. Blue jays don't seem to ever attack the male cardinal, but they will go after the females in a minute. Every time a jay went after one of the female cardinals as she gathered the seeds from the feeder, the male would chase him away. I got tired of the birds and spent a while watching a deer drinking from the other side of the lake. Then I went back to the ripples.

I thought for a long time. I really wanted a drink badly, but I had given my word. And I had given my word to someone who would never tolerate one's failure to keep that word. A beer-drinking, therapist buddy of mine later told me that I had painted myself into that corner on purpose, subconsciously or not, and that I knew that my life depended on success or failure.

I knew I needed to develop a strategy. I knew I was tired of being a drunk. And I knew that I wanted something to drink.

I didn't know this then, but I do now. One of the hardest parts of moving from being a "practicing alcoholic" to being a "reforming alcoholic" is finding something acceptable to drink. This makes sense if one keeps in mind that the practicing alcoholic is used to always having something to drink at hand. I don't think this pattern ever changes. One needs a drink to be passionate about. I considered all of my options for quite a while, mentally striking anything alcoholic, and I finally did one of the smartest things I had done in a long time.

I made a big pot of strong black coffee.

I drank that pot and made another.

For the rest of the afternoon I did only three things:

I drank coffee…

I watched the ripples on the lake…

And I peed on every tree in the yard.

The coffee had started the cleansing process. It is my good friend to this very day.

My friends brought a six pack of beer and put it in the refrigerator.

I asked why and was told, "It's in case you get the d.t.'s."

I told them that a promise was a promise and that if I got the d. t.'s, I would just have to live with it. They left the beer anyway and I allowed it to stay. I decided that the six pack in the refrigerator would be my own personal tempting devil. It was, and it stayed there, too, until I gave it to a friend one Sunday a couple of years later.

Later that night I started sweating. I went to bed and I thought I had caught the flu from someone. The symptoms were the same, nausea, fever, sweats, chills, and not being able to keep any food in my body. I couldn't sleep. I didn't want to stay awake. At one time I looked out the window and thought the fence posts in the horse pasture were police surrounding the house in preparation for taking me to jail for some unknown reason. I lay in the bed alternately freezing and sweating. The sheets were wet. I couldn't get warm. I was burning up hot. I finally went to sleep and dreamed terrible nightmares all night.

The next day, I woke and found myself looking for alcohol but I made friends with the coffee pot instead. I drank coffee in bed and sweated the entire day. I read Louis L'Amour books. Over the next two or three days, I went through my entire sixty volume Louis L'Amour collection and drank ungodly amounts of coffee. The sweating and chills stopped on the third day and then it was just me and Louis and 8 O'clock coffee. In my head, I lived with the cowboys and associated their frontier with the frontier that I was approaching.

And on the fifth day I ate. I ate everything in the house.

Oranges first. Until they were all gone, at which time I attacked the bananas. Then I put a roast on the grill for later and ate a loaf of white bread. Just bread, mind you, no butter, mayo, filler, or anything else. Just bread. The entire loaf.

I made a pot of rice. I made a big, big pot of rice. I ate it all with butter and salt and pepper.

When the roast was almost done, I ate it. I cleaned every morsel of meat from the bone and then broke it open and sucked the marrow out.

I rested.

And then I walked through the greenhouse and the nursery, touching the flowers, stroking the leaves, pinching a top or two here and there, admiring new growth, and making mental notes of problems that needed solving. I felt really good. I felt better than I had felt in a long, long time.

And that was when I knew that I would never, ever drink alcohol again. The dragon was still there. He wasn't dead, but he was down for the count. Dragons like that one never die, but they become easier and easier to live with and to control.

But I promised myself that I would always remember what Bilbo Baggins said. "It does not do to leave a sleeping dragon out of your calculations."

Ponytail drove up with Harce in the car at the end of the second week of our contract. We sat on the porch with a never-ending pot of coffee and talked of our experience. Harce's story was similar to mine and he was anxious to show me what he had done.

"Hey, John, you remember your momma wanted me to line that antique steamer trunk with cedar for her?"

I told him I had trouble forgetting that steamer trunk because Mom asked about it every Sunday morning when I talked to her long distance.

"Well," he said, "I have always had trouble cutting the wood thin enough. So while I was sweating that likker out of my body, I spent a lot of time working on the sawmill blade. I got it sharper than any saw blade has ever been in the whole world – ever."

He grinned and walked out to Ponytail's truck where he pulled out an eight foot long piece of six inch wide cedar. It was cut thin. It was cut so thin that he wrapped it around his shoulders like an old lady's shawl and grinned and yelled, "How's that for cutting it thin? This here wood is so thin it's only got one side."

I was impressed. I knew mom would be pleased with her cedar-lined steamer chest. Eventually, she was.

Harce sat and drank coffee and was really quiet for a while. I could tell something was bothering him. "Hey, John, I ain't had a drink in two weeks, what about you?"

I replied, "I haven't had any alcohol in my body and I don't think I ever will again."

"What about when our bet is over?"

"Harce, I told you – never again. I don't ever want to go through that first week again. Do you understand? I'm ready to get on with my life." He looked me in the eye and nodded.

We sat quietly, drinking coffee. I eventually got up and made another pot, found an extension cord and a table, and moved the coffee maker out on the porch. I set it where the beer cooler used to live. I poured us both a fresh cup.

"You're mighty quiet, Harce. Is something bothering you?"

He turned his head from the lake and looked me dead in the eye. "It's the contract," he said.

I replied, "Well, you haven't had an alcoholic drink in two weeks, have you?"

He looked back at the lake. "No, John, I ain't going to break that part of the contract, but my leg gets to hurting and I get kind of mean like I was brought up and I ain't been treating Louann right. I have an important question about the contract."

I looked at him and raised my eyebrows.

"You see," he started, "I need to know if the contract involves anything but likker and beer."

I thought about it. "Well, as I understand the contract, we both agreed to quit drinking alcoholic beverages until your leg got dealt with. That is my understanding. My understanding is also that either of us can drink alcohol again if we desire after your leg is dealt with." I paused. "Personally, Harce, I don't desire to ever drink alcohol again. The way I feel right now is that it would take a big, big man to hold me down and pour a beer down my throat."

Harce stared at the floor with his elbows propped on his knees. "Is marijuana in the contract?"

I said, "No, I guess it's not. It ought to be, but I guess it's not. A contract is a contract."

He kept staring at the floor. "Well, my leg is getting worse, and I've been back to the doctor and he's right proud of me for not drinking. I asked him if me smoking dope would stop him from working on me and he told me that it was the alcohol he was worried about. He told me that if I told anybody he said this he would call me a liar, but he said that smoking pot could be considered medicinal. I just wanted to be sure it wasn't in the contract. I don't want to break the contract in any way. Grandpa would come back from the dead and haunt me if I did."

I thought long and hard. "Well, Harce, I can't tell you one way or the other. I always told you that pot smoking got in the way of my beer drinking. You never had that problem."

He said, "I could sure use a buzz on and it sure does make the hurting stop."

I replied, "I guess, do what you want. It's not in the contract."

There was a long contemplative silence.

Harce turned to me and said, "You know, John, now that you ain't drinking no more, there ain't nothing to keep you from smoking some dope with me."

I grinned at him. "Harce, there is no way in hell that I plan to replace one bad habit with another."

The dope smoking was not in the contract. I couldn't enforce anything in the contract but the cessation of drinking alcohol.

I always look back and wonder if I could have made a difference in what happened later. I'll never know. I guess, as Harce would have said, "That was yesterday. It is what it is."

chapter 18
SPRING GERANIUMS AND BUD

I guess that growing a crop of geraniums is one of the most satisfying and rewarding endeavors I have ever undertaken. Geraniums are fun. They grow quickly and they are very responsive to good culture. The crop is started somewhere around the end of January when the rooted cuttings come in from the plant broker. They are immediately planted in sterilized six inch pots and placed carefully on the greenhouse bench. The greenhouse has been cleaned with precision and sprayed down with anti-bacterial solutions. Young geraniums are disease-prone but good culture and cleanliness combined with other good growing techniques and experience will provide a crop of the most wonderful plants known to man. It is easy to screw up a crop of geraniums but that year I had the benefit of having screwed up a lot in the past and of having learned from the mistakes. I also had a new advantage: I was sober. That hadn't happened in a long time.

It was an early spring. The geraniums had been planted right on time, fertilized weekly, pruned and pinched for shape, and were just starting to bloom. The inside of the greenhouse had turned into an explosion of red, pink and white flowers which rose gracefully above dark green leaves with their characteristic darker zonal borders. Every morning when I first entered the greenhouse, I was almost overwhelmed, first by the colors and then by the unique fragrance of the geranium plant itself. There is no other smell like it. I had worked hard on the plants through the final stages of the north Georgia winter and they were almost ready for market. Market was almost ready for them. It was a good thing, too, because I was broke. I didn't really worry about being broke, though, because a thousand geraniums in the spring have a way of alleviating this condition. I got up one bright, sunny morning, backed the van up to the greenhouse door, and started loading plants. It was time to fix the urns and planters for some of my best clients.

I had started driving again. During the final years of my drinking experience I had wisely stopped driving for the simple reason that I knew I would probably get in trouble if I drove. Not driving was probably the only smart thing that I did during those years, but now, being sober, I felt confident that I could handle the situation. I practiced on back roads in my old Ford van, getting back my long-lost driving skills and renewing my confidence. Learning to drive the first time was easy because I was invincible when I was sixteen, but learning the second time at fifty five was a frightening experience. I had come face to face with the realization of my mortality. It seemed that every other car on the road was out to get me and that every drainage ditch beckoned the van to its final resting place. I had persevered, though, and soon became the best driver on the road. At least, I was the best in my opinion.

The van wasn't running quite right. My long-time mechanic had just died a couple of weeks before, I was broke, and I knew that I would have to deal with all of this in the next couple of days. I had a plan, though. I would will the van to keep running while I sold some geraniums and then I would find a mechanic and get the van fixed. Being the world's greatest optimist, I knew in my heart that all of this would work. It did, too, but not quite in the manner I expected. I got a new friend out of the deal, though.

I carefully loaded the van with geraniums, picking off any spotted leaf, pinching almost spent blooms, and wiping the pots clean. They were beautiful. I put a hundred plants in the cargo area and stood back, drank a cup of coffee, and grinned bigger than I had grinned in a long time. I had it all worked out: go to the mansion on Mount Alto and plant half of them, and then go visit a few of my florist friends and sell the rest. The check from Mount Alto would be in the mail in a day or two and would pay the bills, and the florists would pay cash so Marsha could buy some much needed groceries. I had a thermos of coffee and thirty dollars.

I had a plan for the day, but things didn't quite work out as I had predicted. To start with, the van was a bit slow starting up. The motor just didn't seem to want to turn over, but finally it fired up and I drove straight up to the Mount Alto estate and made it up the quarter mile twisting and turning driveway. No one was home that day and I took my time, enjoyed the magnificent view, and planted my prized geraniums – fifty of them. I cleaned up, watered the newly planted container garden, drank a cup of coffee and admired my work, cranked the van, and headed out the driveway. I was very happy. I was independently driving and working for the first time in what seemed like forever. It was a beautiful day. I was on my way to impress the florists with my beautiful flowers, and all of my problems would soon be over.

Then everything changed. I stopped at the end of the driveway to move a fallen limb out of the way. The motor in the van quit. I moved the limb and got back in the van, turning the key. Unnnh, unnnnnnnh, rrrrrrruuuunnnh, nothing. Starting to worry, I tried it again: uuunnnnuunnh, nothing. Unnnnnhrrrhuinnh, nothing. One more time: unnnnn hhhhhrrrrnnnnn—And that was when the key twisted off. The entire assembly fell out of the steering wheel post. I sat there looking at the entire ignition assembly which I held in my hand. Cell phones were just starting to gain popularity at the time and I didn't have one. The nearest house was a quarter of a mile uphill and no one was home. I couldn't even roll the van down the mountain because the wheels were twisted to the left and the steering wheel was locked. I got out of the van and looked first to the right, then to the left, up and down Mount Alto Road. No traffic.

A lot of people might have gotten depressed, but not me. I had half a load of geraniums in the back of the van. I opened the back doors, looked in and grinned. I gathered up an armload of plants, holding them so that my chin was covered with reds and pinks and whites, and stood on the side of the road at the end of the driveway. After a few minutes, lady in a Mercedes drove by, stopped, backed up, rolled her window down and said, "Are you selling those plants or just standing there looking good?"

I said, "These plants are for the first nice person who comes along and allows me to make two calls on her cell phone."

She laughed and immediately handed me a cell phone. I opened the back door and set the plants on the back floor of the Mercedes. Both of us were happy.

I called and got the number for Perry's wrecker service. I called Perry, made arrangements for a "rollback" tow truck, said my goodbyes and thanks to the lady in the Mercedes, and sat down next to a tree to wait. It was my lucky day. Everything was going to be all right.

And everything did turn out all right. It was my lucky day. Perry was out sick that day and he sent a new driver to take care of me.

"Shane," he stated, shaking my hand. "Perry told me you were 'John the plant man' and that I should take good care of you." I appreciated that.

And Shane was good. Since the transmission and wheels were locked down, he had to actually drag the van up on the platform of the truck. He worked hard and gave me careful instructions to keep the van in a straight line as he loaded it. I have always admired craftsmen, and Shane was really good at his job. I pondered. "Can a really good tow truck driver be classified as a 'craftsman?'" I figured out that the answer was "yes he can."

After the van had been firmly fastened with all manner of chains, I grabbed my thermos of coffee and got in the tow truck with Shane. He turned to me and asked, "Where to?"

I hesitated, thinking of an answer. If I took the van to my house, I would end up with another tow bill eventually. I gave Shane my last thirty dollars for the towing bill and kept thinking.

I looked over at the driver, patiently awaiting my answer. "I don't know where to go. My mechanic of many years just died. Do you know someone who can fix it?"

Shane replied, "My dad can fix it. You know him, don't you? His name is Bud Sims."

The name was familiar; I had heard about Bud, but never met him. I asked, "Isn't he the chicken fighter?"

Shane laughed. "He calls himself one, but he's actually a better mechanic."

"Sounds like a good place to go as far as I'm concerned," I replied.

And that's how I met Bud.

We went down Mount Alto Road, turned left on Horseleg Creek Road, out the bypass, turned into Bell's Ferry Road on the side where it had been shut off on account of the bypass when they built it, and then made a left on Berwin Road.

"I haven't ever been here before." I had to shout because of the noise a train was making as it went by.

Shane looked over at me as he navigated the curves on the narrow road that was only wide enough for a car and a half. "This used to be Berwin. It's where the trains going one direction pull over to the side and let a train going in the other direction go by. It used to be the last 'whistle stop' and mail pick-up station before the county seat. Now, it's just my dad and some trailers with the train running through the back yards. It's good, though, because there cain't nobody else build anything back there on account of the train, so it's pretty private." He slowed down and pulled over almost into a ditch in order to let a pick up truck pulling a trailer with a John Deere tractor pass by. "The train makes a bunch of noise, but it's ok because my old man and his buddies talk a lot. They have learned that they can either yell louder than the train or they can shut up while it goes by and figure out what they are going to say next. They don't never seem to run out of something to say in between trains." He paused, pulled over to the side of the road, and said, "Here it is."

And there it was. A concrete block building sat at the bottom of a hill. There were three bays with garage doors, a collection of cars and trucks parked off to the side, two big dogs of some kind of breed or the other quietly watching the tow truck, and a short, skinny man with curly grey hair, shiny blue eyes, and the biggest, warmest grin I ever saw. Off to the side of the shop was a plowed garden spot just waiting to be planted, and way off to the left stood a small but neat wood and block house with porches all over the place and a giant oak tree out front.

The curly-headed guy yelled, "Way to go, Shane, you brought me some more business!"

Another loud train went by as we yelled introductions. I had now formally met Bud.

Bud checked out the situation with the van, crawled up under the dash board, reaching a place where a slightly larger man would have gotten stuck, and unlocked the transmission and steering wheel. Shane was impressed. Bud shook his finger at Shane and said, "I done showed you and showed you how to do that. You probly could of done it, too, if you hadn't gone and gotten so damn fat." I decided I kind of liked this guy.

Bud checked out the problem with the van, assured me that he could fix it, and kind of started figuring out how much it would cost. I figured it was time to give him the bad news.

"I just gave Shane all of my money for the towing," I said. "I won't have any more until I sell those geraniums, and I can't do that until I have the van running."

Bud had obviously heard such sob stories before. He grinned. "What's a geranium?"

I opened the back door of the van and pointed.

"You talking about them flars?"

"Yeah, those are geraniums. I sell them to the florists and plant them at people's houses."

Bud turned and looked at his front porch. "It's about time to set 'em out, ain't it?"

I told him what I had done on the mountain that morning.

Bud looked at me, looked at his porch, and then looked back at me. "Why don't you fix up my porch like you did for that rich lady while I work on your truck? You got flars like them, you don't need no money."

I looked at him with hesitation, "Bud, are you sure?"

Shane laughed.

Bud laughed and said, "My boy there, he's laughing 'cause he knows and I know that you just met one trading sumbitch. That's me. I'd rather trade and deal than fight chickens and that's a bunch." He didn't lie, either. I found out later.

DANCING

I didn't see Harce for a while, but I did hear things. I ran into Sobrina, the marijuana dealer, at the Magic Market and she told me that Harce had surprised everybody by quitting drinking. She said, "He ain't had a drop to drink that I could tell, but he's trying to smoke up all the weed this side of Atlanta, and he's been seeing a lot of the doctor lately. They're making sure he don't have no infection. He sure is uptight, though, and he ain't treating Louann real good. She still sneaks around and gets some beer and Harce yells at her about it. He has started yelling at her about everything. Louann puts her hands on her hips and puts her head sideways – You know what I mean, like this? And then Louann tells him something like, 'I didn't promise nobody nothing.' But she keeps cooking and cleaning for him and the other thing, too. I don't know why, but she does."

I also ran into Randolph who owns the liquor store. He looked at me funny and said, "John, I heard you and Harce quit drinking. I believe it, too. My sales are down 20%."

A few days later the phone rang. I answered.

"Hey, John," the voice said. "This here's Harce."

"Where'd you get the phone?" I asked. "You don't ever call me unless you're in jail."

"I may as well be in jail. I'm in the hospital down here in

Atlanta and they won't let me smoke or cuss or do nothing. But I got a problem."

"What would that be?" I asked cautiously.

"They're fixing to take my leg off and I told them I lost it in a bet and they got to save it so I can pay off the bet. The nurses and the doctors keep telling me they can't do that and it don't matter how mad I get or how much hell I raise, they ain't going to let me pay the debt. I told them it was all about honor, and all they do is laugh."

I kind of thought it was funny, too. I could picture Harce bringing me his leg in a pickle jar of formaldehyde with a grin on his face. Somehow, it didn't matter to me if he paid that particular debt or not. "It will be all right, Harce," I replied. "I think that when I see you without the leg, I will know whether it got gone or not."

There was a long pause, "You going to have to do something, John. I shook on it. I got to pay off."

I told him I would do everything I could. I coughed a bit to cover the laughing fit.

"And, there's one more thing, John."

"What's that?"

"Are you going to come visit me in the hospital?"

I thought a moment. "Harce, if I were in the hospital, would you come see me?"

"Naw, I hate hospitals. I know damn well I wouldn't come see you."

"I feel the same."

Harce laughed. "I don't blame you none. If you come see me, I'll have to come see you some time and I'd rather not be obligated. I'll tell you what. If you don't come see me once, I get to not come see you twice. Fair deal?"

"Fair deal."

End of conversation.

I didn't have much to do that day, so I cleaned out my grill. I went to see Harce's doctor and gave him a package. "I'll never tell anyone I gave you this, doc." I told him. He and I had a short conversation about the package and I left.

Two weeks later, as I sat at the work table in the yard carefully pruning a bonsai tree, I heard the peculiar rattles and thumps that told me Ponytail was coming up the driveway. The black Chevy S-10 dodged the dogs, stopped, and Ponytail climbed out the driver's side window. Acting like an important chauffer, he walked to the other side of the truck and bowed as he opened the door. Harce's left foot emerged. He used Ponytail for support and hauled himself up. He grabbed onto the pickup and reached in the back to pull out an old wooden crutch. He had a big grin on his face as he moved over to where I was working and pulled up a chair. The dogs sniffed a lot. They were used to seeing Harce, but there was something different, it seemed. Right there, below the knee where there was once a foot, there was nothing. I looked at his leg. I looked him in the eye. "Well, Harce," I asked, "other than that, how did you like your trip to Atlanta?"

He started to say something and thought a bit before figuring out that my question was pretty funny. He laughed. "I'm here to pay my debt."

He handed me a box. I opened it and pulled out a beautiful handmade sugar bowl. It was glazed with browns and golds and here and there a touch of cobalt blue. The top was fastened with wax and a couple of pieces of duct tape. I turned it over and looked on the bottom where I saw a little circle with "HC" stamped in the middle. I didn't let on that it was the same package I had given the doctor.

I was impressed. "Where did you get this? It's beautiful craftsmanship."

Harce grinned. "I traded a bottle of shine for it one time. Got it from a crazy guy. He said he made it, but I don't really know. I forgot his name. Anyway, my leg is in there. My doctor here in town understood that I needed to pay off our bet, so he got them to cremate my leg and he gave it to me in a baggie. It looked kind of like cocaine or charcoal ash or something like that and I put it in that sugar bowl so you would be happy. And now I know the debt is paid so I don't have to worry about it. That doctor sure did think it was funny, though." Harce got out his "fixin's" and started rolling a joint. He told me that he had an appointment with a doctor who was going to make him a fake leg in three weeks. He studied the bonsais, smoked his marijuana, yelled at Ponytail and they left. I didn't see Harce again for about six weeks.

I was really busy with my flower planting business that year. Since I had quit drinking alcohol and started trying to drink all the coffee in Columbia, I had an immense surge of energy. It showed up in the form of self confidence, focus on the job, quality of work, and creativity. Also, I was in the process of learning something that I finally put into words: "When you quit drinking, you find out who your friends are." After the first Sunday or two, my drinking friends stopped showing up in the afternoons to "talk." One reason, I think, was that there was no longer a cooler of Sunday beer sitting on the porch. The other reason was that people are uneasy drinking alcoholic beverages around someone who has quit. To illustrate, my mother and I had been invited to dinner with some nice people. I felt like something was wrong and finally I told them so. "There's something wrong here." I stated.

"What is it?" asked the hostess with concern.

"You all usually have a glass of wine for dinner and this time you are not."

The atmosphere got a bit uncomfortable. I heard phrases such as: "Well, we thought . . ." and "Well, you know we didn't want to . . ." and so on. That's when Mom came through. She stood up with her hands on her hips and said, "It's like this. John has money in his pocket, he has a driver's license and a car, and there's a beer store on every corner. If he wants to drink, he can." I loved her for that. But, I digress.

A few weeks later on a beautiful day when Marsha was in her garden picking some tomatoes and peppers and I had the grill going just right and was in the process of roasting and peeling the produce to get it ready for a big batch of salsa, Ponytail and Harce showed up. I waited for Ponytail to get the crutch and watched as Harce stuck his left leg out of the passenger's side. I noticed that he had shorts on for the first time since I met him. Then it appeared. Where the stump had been on his other leg was a bright blue apparition with a foot shaped plate on the bottom. Harce jumped out of the truck and danced a jig. "Look here, John. Look here, Marsha. I can dance."

We were really impressed. I examined the new apparatus at length. It was polished to a high gloss and if I kind of let go of the fact that it was a fake leg, I could see a lot of beauty in it. Harce was really happy.

"It was kind of like a hardware store where the guy worked. They had every kind of nuts and bolts and parts and, man, they had these tools like I never seen. And that doctor, he really knew how to use them tools. This guy, he was working titanium and steel like I would work a piece of wood. He used a torch to heat it, then he cut and drilled, then he polished it. I really wanted to get my hands on them tools, and he knew it, too, he showed me how everything worked, but when it came to welding, he made me sit in the corner. Man, I kept thinking that I could of made a good living doing that stuff and really loved it."

Harce leaned back in the chair and rubbed the place where the prosthesis joined his knee. "It gets a little sore real quick, 'specially when I dance," he observed, "but the doctor said it would get better as time goes by." He studied the leg a bit, very carefully. "I watched the leg guy, and I think I'm going to put me a little door right here where the ankle would be. I can make a sliding door sort of thing and have a good place to hide my pot. Won't nobody find it there."

I thought he was joking. I was wrong.

Harce got tired of talking about his leg and we just sat there and stared at the lake for a while. I could tell something was on his mind. He started. "You know, John, I been out of work for a while and I got bills to pay."

I thought, "That's what I was afraid of. Here it comes." But I was wrong. I should have known better.

He continued, "I been trying and trying to figure out how to make some money. I'm just getting to where I can work, and everybody has been really good to me and done for me but I'm still behind. I met this guy in the hospital . . ." He sat and stared out at the ripples on the lake. "There was this guy I met in the hospital and he makes good money getting people married."

I asked, "Is he a preacher?"

"Naw, he don't marry people, he gets people married. See what I mean? I mean he finds people in Mexico City that want to come to the States legally and then he finds somebody to marry them and makes it happen. And he only deals with high class people with money."

I looked up from the ripples. "Sounds illegal to me."

"The guy in Atlanta told me that it was probably illegal but that if you did it right, everything would come out ok. Then he met Louann and told me that he would give me five thousand dollars if I would get Louann to marry a guy and that they could both still live at my house and Louann could still take care of me if you know what I mean and that after a while, Louann and the guy could get a divorce and me and Louann could go on like nothing ever happened. He even said the Mexican guy would pay room and board while he lived with me."

Harce stopped and looked at me. I must have had a really funny look on my face. This was more than I could take in at one sitting. All kinds of repercussions, legal and otherwise, were running through my mind. I just sat there with my eyebrows raised all the way up past my receding hairline and my mouth hanging open.

"Anyway," he continued, "anyway, I cain't see nothing wrong with it and I keep on trying and trying to figure out a reason not to do it. And that money and that room and board would solve a lot of problems for me."

I just stared at him.

"And you cain't tell nobody I told you about this, either, John. I just wanted you to know what I was thinking."

I was still staring at the ground shaking my head slowly when Harce went home.

I could swear that I had smelled beer on his breath.

chapter 20 PORE

My son Paul and his girlfriend, Edna, had come to visit and were sitting on the couch. Bud and I had been talking about the Boston butts that I had put on the grill, and when they showed up Bud had gotten that look in his eye that I knew so well. I introduced Bud to Edna and she was polite. We talked about this and that for a couple of minutes until I said, "Bud, how pore was your family when you were growing up?" Bud grew silent and got a sad, thoughtful look on his face. Paul and Edna waited politely for his answer.

Bud kind of scratched his wooly white hair. "Well," he said, looking at his knees, "Well, we was pore. I remember one year Daddy had worked at the sawmill til planting time and he saved enough money for to buy a pig. He told us that we would grow that pig big and fat and have it for Christmas. And that's what we did. Daddy kept saying that for once we wasn't going to be hungry for Christmas. He kept saying that we would kill that hog on December 22 and we would have the best Christmas ever.

"Well, that pig turned into a hog and we fed it everything we could think of that it would eat. We fed it table scraps when we had some and we fed it instead of us some of the time. That hog got fatter and fatter."

Bud kind of paused and looked off into space. "Then when

October got here, we didn't have nothing to eat but beans and gravy day after day. We got pretty tarred of beans and gravy but that was all we had to eat, so we got by. Every night after dinner, me and my brother and Daddy would go sit out on the porch and watch that hog get fat, and he got fatter and fatter. We would talk about what a feast we would have come Christmas.

"And then one day when we was really getting tarred of beans and gravy, Daddy looked at me and said, 'Bud, get your brother.' And I got Herman and Daddy got a butcher knife and a dish pan and we follered him out to the hog pen.

"Daddy said, 'Bud, you and Herman throw that hog down on his side and hold him.' And we did and Daddy cut a big ole piece of meat off of his back ham portion. Then he pulled a needle and thread out of his pocket and sewed that hog up as neat as you ever seen. We had some good meat and beans for a couple of days."

Edna looked concerned and asked, "What happened then? Was the hog all right?"

Bud paused again and scratched his head, looking down at the floor. He looked up and said, "Now, that hog was healed up perfect by Christmas and we killed him and ate him. That was shore enough one big old hog."

Before anyone could get over the story, Bud started up again. "You know, when we weren't growing nothing in the winter time, we worked at the sawmill. That started in January and it was cold and the hog was done all et up. Now, we had to have lunch 'cause we worked awful hard moving them logs around and Mama would pack a lunch in a tote bag she done made out of a croker sack. You know, that burlap kind of seed bag, that's a croker sack. Well, the first day she packed my lunch, it was corn bread and turnips. Everybody would go to the shed, it was kind of like that shed you got out in the back yard, naw, maybe a little bit bigger. I think it was bigger.

"Anyhow, we went and put our lunches on a shelf in that little shed and when the whistle blew at dinner time, we would go get our lunch and some water from the spring and we would get 20 minutes to eat. We didn't do much talking neither, we was hungry. After we had et, we went back to work til dark.

"Well, that lunch made of turnips and corn bread was all right for a while, but it started to get old after about a month or so. I couldn't complain, though, 'cause we was all broke and everybody brought whatever lunch they could. Some of the men swapped lunches but I was embarrassed and didn't want them to know that all I had was cornbread and turnips.

"One day, though, I was really, really tarred of cornbread and turnips and I got done a few minutes early with my work so I went to the shed and decided to swap lunches. I got my tote bag and looked at all of them lunches. I fount the heaviest one in the shed and swapped mine for it and run down to a old oak tree and set under it and reached down in the bag to see what I got."

Edna was staring at him. "What was in it?"

Bud kind of grinned. "A hammer and two walnuts."

chapter 21 GETTING READY

I had thought about it and I was having trouble getting the information about Louann marrying the Mexican out of my mind. A couple of days later, Ponytail and Harce paid me a visit and I was able to clarify things.

"Harce, you're talking about asking Louann to *MARRY* someone else?"

"Yeah, man," he replied. "See, I need a bunch of money to pay the bills that I wasn't able to pay when I was getting my leg worked on – right?"

"Right."

"And I still cain't work much 'til I get my leg better and get to where I am more comfortable with it—right?"

"Right."

"And this Mexican guy wants to give me a bunch of money to get Louann to marry him so he can get to work in the States legal – right?"

"Right."

"And so I will get the money for letting her marry him and then he will have to live at our house and pay room and board. He will have to live here because the immigration people will probably watch him for a while to make sure that we ain't just putting on a wedding to get him a green card which we are but if he lives here and all for a while, and if he works and pays his taxes, it will all work out in about a year, and he and Louann can get a divorce and he can go away and I will be able to go back to work by then and me and Louann can be like we were. And while he lives here he can sleep in the other bedroom and Louann can sleep with me like we always done and everything will be all right. Right?"

I didn't answer.

"You ain't saying much, John. Tell me, what do you think?"

I sat there in what I had started to call my "Harce pose," which consisted of my putting my elbows on my knees, staring at the ground between my feet and shaking my head slowly from side to side with a funny halfway grin on my face. The funny halfway grin said that I didn't know whether to laugh or cry. Finally I looked up. "But, Harce, when you think of the possible repercussions—"

"Reper....what? Are you cussing, John?"

Time to rephrase. "When you think of all the things that could go wrong and if you take into consideration all of the emotional, personal, economic and legal issues—"

"John, that's too many damn words. I just wanted you to tell me it would be all right. That's all I'm asking. I need the money."

"Well, Harce," I said, "You sound like you are going to do it anyway, no matter what I say. What's Louann's attitude?"

"Louann don't care. She'll do whatever I tell her to. At least, she always has. Anyway, you'll really like Manuel. He's a mason and he can lay stone and brick and build houses and walls and all kinds of stuff. I might even be able to teach him how to run the saw mill. It's too dangerous for somebody with a fake leg." Harce stopped and thought a while. "And just think of the party we can have. We can have a party like The Colons ain't never seen before. I got the gazebo finished for the wedding chapel and we can have a wedding party and we can celebrate my leg at the same time."

Harce looked at his watch. "I got to go, now. Me and Ponytail got to pick Manuel up at the Greyhound station. I'll let you know what happens."

Harce got in the truck with Ponytail and left. All I could do was sit there and think about what would be going through Manuel's mind as his day developed. I made a pot of coffee and pruned some bonsai trees. Pruning bonsai trees has a tendency to free one's mind.

I had decided to use the following Saturday morning to relax and to see if I could somehow conjure up a positive balance in my checking account. I was running short on money and coffee. It was not meant to be – the relaxing, that is. At about 7:30, I heard the telltale broken muffler and fender-rattling sounds of Ponytail's S-10 pickup truck making its way around the potholes in the driveway. I knew it must be something important because I had long ago established a rule that no one was allowed to show up at my house before 8:30 in the morning. I walked out with my mug of super coffee to see what was going on.

Ponytail got out of the truck. "Harce wants you to c-c-c come ss-s-s-see him."

"What in the hell does he want at this time of the morning on a Saturday?"

"H-h-h he s sss said he w w w wwould give you a –hh-h hunnert dollars. He s sss s ss said h-he has the c c cc-coffee on the grill and bbring your p pp p ppaint g-g-gun"

Harce knew me well enough to know that a hundred dollars would get my attention. I didn't know where he'd gotten it, but I did know that if he sent word that he had the money, he was telling the truth. The paint gun reference got my attention, also. The paint gun is a handle with a trigger that holds a can of upside-down marking paint like the utility people use to mark water, power and phone lines. For years, I had used the paint gun to lay out flower and shrub beds and to help potential clients without a vision get one. The paint gun had been one of my favorite tools for years. I had developed the ability to walk through a yard and paint a circle meaning "tree here," or an X "take this out," or to paint a sweeping "S" curve and say, "take out the grass from here to the pavement and put in a raised flower bed." Harce had seen me do it many times.

I got dressed, poured up my "to go" large insulated coffee cup, fetched the paint gun and a couple of cans of florescent orange marking paint from the barn, crossed my fingers as I started the Ford van and headed toward The Colons. I was totally unprepared for what I saw on my arrival. Several pickup trucks were parked in front of the barn. I could see lots of activity in the front and side yards and more around the gazebo. Louann was yelling something at somebody – I couldn't tell what or at whom. Harce stood at the end of the driveway grinning with a hundred dollar bill in one hand and a large cup of coffee in the other. That suited me.

"All damn hell has broke loose around here," he said nervously. "I don't know what got into Louann, but she's a different person. She's even got Kickstand skeered to death and he ain't generally skeered of nothing."

I got out of the truck and accepted the offerings. The money was good and I slipped it into the front pocket of my jeans, but the coffee was wonderful. There is nothing like a steaming mug of hot, black coffee that was made in an old iron coffee pot over an open wood fire. It smelled like Luzianne with chicory. I burned a blister on my tongue to start with and then decided it was "sipping coffee."

Harce laughed when I burned my tongue and then told me the plan. "Louann said if we was going to have a wedding and a party, we was going to do it as good as the rich folks. She wants you to lay out some flower beds and pathways and tell everybody what to do."

He paused, lost in confused thought. "At least, that's what she said. She's doing a real good job of telling everybody what to do all by herself. I've been hiding as much as I could. Hell, all I did was mention the word 'wedding' and she done went crazy."

I stood and looked at the scene. Kickstand was down on his hands and knees in front of the barbecue pit. As I listened to Louann, I immediately noticed that she was not using "like" or "don't you know" in her sentence construction. I guess she had found a purpose in life and was reborn.

Louann had her hands on her hips as she yelled, "Kickstand, you stay down there and you get every damn one of them cigarette butts up from there. Then you go over there and get every one of them cigarette butts from in front of the damn gazebo." She turned a quick one-eighty. "Ponytail, you get every one of them beer cans and put them in the back of your truck and when you get finished with that, you get all them Rolling Rock bottles and put them in the back of Kickstand's truck. That man at the recycle place ain't gon' know what hit him."

She turned and saw Harce and me staring. She walked in our direction, talking as she approached. "Harce, I don't know where Manuel is hiding, but you go find him and I want him to help John. He's a good guy for a Mexican, but he can out-hide any man I ever seen."

She turned to me, smiling. Her voice moderated and she got sweet and nice. I found that kind of scary. "John, I want you to mark out a bunch of places and then get Manuel and anybody else you need to help. I want you to make flower beds and pathways and stuff like that like you do for the rich folks. If Harce ain't give you enough money, I'll make him give you some more. I want this place perfect." She looked at the ground and repeated softly, "perfect."

She looked back up at me. "You know how you make them garden beds with compost and rocks? Well Manuel is a genius with rocks and he will do the work. You just tell them what to do and if you need any more help I'll get these damn rednecks to pitch in. After that's done, I want to go to your greenhouse and get a bunch of flower plants and I will plant them myself."

About that time, Harce came out from behind the barn with his hand tightly holding the collar of a nice looking-gentleman of Mexican persuasion. "John, this is Manuel. He don't speak no English but for three words, but he is the best mason I ever seen. He can do stone, brick, cultured stone, build slate patios. His visa is about to expire and he's got to do something to get legal. He's a pretty good guy, too. He's gon' help you."

Manuel smiled and shook my hand.

I looked at Manuel and smiled. "¿Habla poquito Ingles?"

He nodded and grinned. "Si, tres palavras."

"Three words?" I asked. "What are they? ¿Que es?"

Manuel was proud of himself and replied in perfect English. "Straight, plumb, level."

I laughed out loud. Those were the only words a really good

mason needed.

I had a pretty good day. I studied the situation and painted lines for two flower beds. I only had to show Manuel once what I wanted. We (meaning "he") hauled in several wheelbarrows of compost and raked it out into a nice curved bed about 8 inches high. Then we (he) went out in the field and picked up several wheelbarrow loads of rocks – God knows, there were plenty of them. I started laying the rocks for the flower bed border to show Manuel how to do it and he pushed me out of the way and took apart what I had done and showed *me* how to do it. I had never seen such a perfect job. In ten minutes Manuel taught me more about laying rock than I had learned in the last ten years. I thought, "Well, I *used to* think I was a good rock man."

What a day. I had never seen a landscaping job go together like that. Louann saw what was going on and rounded up the rednecks. She had three wheelbarrows and a pickup truck at her disposal.

"All right, Kickstand, Ponytail, Rooster, you guys take these wheelbarrows out there and get rocks for Manuel. If you don't get the right rocks, you gon' have to take them back, so be careful." She turned and hollered, "Jeffrey, you and Bobby Joe get Harce's pickup and get the pitchfork and go back behind the saw mill and haul me some compost. I'll tell you when to stop."

I don't know who was more amazed at the activity – me or Manuel. He obviously wasn't used to having help like this and he set out to embarrass the rednecks. The flower beds and pathways were being built almost as fast as I could draw them out with my paint gun. Every once in a while, Manuel would put forth a superhuman effort and catch up. When this happened, he would stand up straight with his hands in the air and shout, "Arriba, Arriba, mas rapido, mas rapido."

Then Louann would holler, "I don't know what the hell that means, but you guys better do it anyhow."

The entire yard was being rapidly transformed into something that would have graced the cover of the *Redneck Southern Living* – if there was one.

Progress on the landscaping project was going so well that Louann allowed a beer break every thirty minutes. She kept my coffee coming, also. Harce must have gotten a really good deposit on his contract because I noticed about ten cases of beer in the corner of the barn. One of Louann's friends had started a fire and was cooking lunch. It smelled good. During one of the breaks, Harce approached me. "John, where, exactly, does our beer drinking contract stand?"

I thought about it. "I guess we both did what we said we were going to do and you have your new leg and you're not going to die from the old one and I have the ashes at my house. I guess the contract is done."

He looked at me. "Then, can I drink some beer?"

"I guess so, if you want to. You ought to think about it, though."

"I done thought about it. I just wanted to make sure I kept my word."

I thought a moment. "Well, Harce, a contract is a contract." I thought for another moment. "But, you know, Harce, this thing with the wedding is already out of hand and I got to thinking about the contracts involved and I wonder how you are going to handle them."

Harce got a quizzical look on his face. "I only got one contract. That's with the Mexican. It says that I will let Louann marry Manuel and stay married until it is ok for him to stay in the States."

I smiled and held up a finger. "If you think about it, the marriage is a contract with God. How are you going to handle that? It looks to me like you are entering a contract with the intention of breaking it. Think on that."

Harce looked at me long and hard, then he said, "I'll think about that part of it later. Right now, I done took some of the Mexican's money and we shook on it. I cain't back out of that."

"I just wanted to make you aware of it," I said.

Then Harce grinned. "Well, that other contract says I can drink a beer, right?"

"Right."

"Well, I'm gon' go get me one. You want a beer, John?"

"No, Harce. I have another contract."

"A beer-drinking contract? Who you got it with?"

"With me."

"Oh."

There was a wonderful lunch break and everyone was proud of the work that was getting done. I was stuffing myself with magnificent barbecue and reaching for a jalapeno pepper to follow it up when Louann came and sat down beside me.

"John, now I want you to finish painting the lines and me and you and Ponytail will go to your greenhouse and load the van up with flowers and plants. Then, the flower beds will be ready and I'll plant them tomorrow. I think the wedding will be in two weeks."

So that's what we did. Louann was rather quiet while we traveled and loaded the van. On the way back, though, she said, "You know, I know Harce told me this is just a wedding to make it where Manuel can stay in Georgia, and I think that anybody who wants to work ought to be able to work anywhere they want to, and all that. But, you know? I ain't never had nobody marry me and this is probably gon' be the only wedding I ever get to have, and, you know, I just want it to be a nice one. You understand, don't you?"

I had a ten dollar gift card from Ace Hardware and they were having a sale. I didn't really need anything because I had fixed my toilet the day before, but I thought I'd look around anyway. They had a table full of different items for one dollar. I saw some very nice desk calculators and picked up four of them – one for Bud, one for me, and a couple of extras. I talked with this old lady about how my first calculator cost a week's pay. There was a nice packet of scissors that I picked out to use on the finer bonsai pruning. I walked away from the display.

Then I had a thought. There were some neat packages of crayons – twenty four to the package, and some notebooks. I went back to the display and picked up a package of crayons and a package of notebooks for each of Bud's grandchildren – Chloe, Nathan, and Emily. They love it when I bring them things. It doesn't matter what it is. One time I took them a tube of live crickets—but that's another story.

On the way home, I stopped at Bud's house with a bag full of stuff. It turned out that the children were spending some rare time with their mother and Bud was sitting on his front porch with his shoes off, grinning. I took a seat in the three legged chair because Herman, the rooster, won't allow anyone but Helen to sit on the porch swing. I handed Bud the calculator and he had a fit. He loved it. Then I gave him the bag and said, "I brought this here stuff for the grandyoungguns."

He looked inside and said, "Aw, hell, now how in the hell did you know it was Chloe's birthday? I ain't told nobody. We're having her party tomorrow." I thought it best to just grin and not say anything.

Bud got me and him a glass of tea and we talked for a while about the best way to sharpen a chain saw. We didn't sharpen one, mind you, we just talked about it.

Yankee drove up. I knew Yankee didn't own a car, but Bud told me it was Yankee's daughter's car and he used it whenever she fell asleep and left the keys laying out. He said Yankee's daughter would kick his ass when he got home 'cause she didn't like him to drive it. Yankee had on a pair of sweat pants shorts. That's all. He came up and sat on the porch swing but then thought better of it when the rooster explained who the swing belonged to. Yankee moved to the porch steps.

I asked Bud how he planned to spend the rest of the day and this was the conversation: "Well, they's having a motorcycle ride this evening and I thought I might go to it."

"I thought you sold your bike," I observed.

"Yeah, I did. I got to needing some money. I sure did like that bike. But anyhow, Luke Burkett – he's the preacher that got fired from Morrison Springs Baptist Church. You know him, don't you Yankee?"

Yankee owned up that he did.

"Well," Bud continued, "well, ol' Luke told me I could get his Harley out of his barn and use it. I like going on them rides. It'll be a bunch of people. Everybody loves the bug run. They like it 'cause you don't know who won till you get to the Sonic over there on the Alabama Road. Last time, I won two hunnert and sixty dollars." He took a sip of tea and looked off into the distance.

I know better than to interrupt Bud when he gets to this point, so I took a sip of tea and waited.

Bud grinned and started up again. "They start at Cave Spring and then they go up to Cedar Bluff, and they cut off through the backwaters like you're going to Fort Payne. It's a bunch of motorcycles and it makes a bunch of noise and they do it so it gets dark right about in the middle of it. Before they start, they put one of them little round yellow stickers in the middle of everybody's headlight. It costses five dollars to get that sticker put on there. Then all them people get their motorcycles crunk and they start off. Sometimes we have a po-lice escort.

"After we get up to the hills around Fort Payne, we take a back road that comes out on the Alabama Road down there by The Narrows. Then we head on to the Sonic and meet up in that big old empty parking lot where the Wal-Marts used to be. That's where they have the final judging on the bug run."

"Is it some kind of race?" I asked.

Yankee snorted like he was trying not to laugh.

"You don't know what a bug run is, John?" Bud asked. "Well, see when we get to the Sonic, one guy goes around and puts your number on your yellow sticker. They used to do it with names until they tried to fit Luke Burkett's name on his sticker and there weren't room. Now they use numbers. Last year I was number thirteen. I didn't like it much, but it turned out to be my lucky number." He took a sip of tea.

"Then they peel off your sticker and take it over to the measuring table and the one with the dead bug the closest to the center wins the pot. Fifty fifty, the organization gets half and the winner gets half. I won two hundred and sixty dollars. The biker organization gives lots of money to charities like the homeless shelter and other stuff. Sometimes they just figure out somebody to help and help them. I think they're trying to change the image of bikers.

"Actually, last year before the judging, I told Luke Burkett and Steve Johnson– you know Steve Johnson, don't you? He's the one with his fingers cut off, I know you know him. Anyway, I told them we should agree to split but Steve Johnson said he weren't giving a third of his money to nobody – kind of like he had already won. So when I won, I weren't going to split with nobody. They all wanted to go to Hooter's and figured I could buy them some beer but I told them I don't drink beer and I ain't buying no beer. I bought them all a coke but they didn't want them so I drank three cokes while they drank up all the beer they could afford and looked at them pretty girls in them short shorts.

"I got tired of listening to them drunk sumbitches and so I got one of them girls to the side and pointed at Steve Johnson– you know he ain't all there, don't you, John – and I told that pretty girl that it was Steve Johnson's birthday.

"Well, you should of seed it. Three or four of them girls went up to him like he was good looking or something and one of them started massaging his shoulders and ol' Steve got this look on his face like he was really special. Then they pulled up this table and got him to stand up on it and hold a salt shaker in each hand and told him just how to shake them in time and they started singing Happy Birthday kind of rock and roll like. It took Steve Johnson a little while to figure out what was going on and all them bikers was laughing their asses off. Finally, Steve said, 'Wait jest a damn minute. It ain't my birthday. Who done this? I'll kick his butt.'"

Bud laughed, "He warn't gon catch me, though, I was headed out the door."

chapter 23
BRUISES

Louann stood alone on the porch with a bruise on her face and a hummingbird on her shoulder. I watched in amazement as the hummingbird flew to the flower bed, serviced a few salvia blooms, and returned to her shoulder. I decided to ignore the bruise.

"I brought you some hanging baskets for the gazebo, Louann."

"Thanks, John, I'll look at them in a minute after Biscus gets through eating."

"Biscus?" I watched the hummingbird fly over to the pink honeysuckle vine.

"He's my pet hummingbird," she replied. "He likes to play a while in the mornings."

The hummingbird flew back to her shoulder. She turned and smiled at the bird and said, "Hi, Biscus."

I sat down on the porch swing and stared.

Watching Louann and the bird interact became an experience in meditation. She sat down in the handcrafted cedar chair and silently watched Biscus as he moved quickly from shoulder to flower to shoulder. She had a gentle Mona Lisa type smile on her face. I knew the smile wasn't a grin because she didn't want me to see her teeth. Otherwise, it would have been a big grin.

"I really like Biscus, you know," she said quietly. "He's been with me almost all his life." She stopped and quietly watched him for a moment. "I found him on the porch one morning. He wasn't as big as a dime, you know. He was almost dead. I don't know where the nest was, but Biscus had probly fallen out and he was about to die. I didn't know what to do, but I knew the other hummingbirds liked sugar water, so I scooped him up and got an eyedropper and some sugar water and I put it up to his little beak and he moved. I was glad he wasn't dead."

She smiled big and held up her finger for the hummingbird. He landed on her finger and waited while she moved her hand to her shoulder. "He'll get tired and take a nap in a tree in a few minutes," she said. "He moves so fast that he is either eating or sleeping. But he don't never, never yell at me. That's what I like. He don't never, never yell at me."

Louann continued, "Anyway, that was a couple of years ago and it was in the late spring when I found Biscus. I fed him and took care of him and he grew up pretty fast and then he started going out and working on the red salvia. You see that big red hibiscus bloom over there? Well, that's what he liked the best. That's why I called him Biscus, so I could say, "hi, Biscus.""

She paused and smiled and watched as Biscus flew out to the perennial blue salvia and returned to her shoulder.

"I learned about giving my pets the right names from my friend Mary. Mary went to college and she comes around to get tomatoes sometimes. I had this Siamese fighting fish one time and I didn't know what to name him. Mary told me that the fish was really called a 'Beta' and that its name should be 'Alphie.' I don't really know why, but it sounded good. She told me that Alphie and Beta went together. Then, when she was leaving, she looked at the fish and asked it 'what's it all about, Alphie' and then she laughed. I didn't know why that was funny. Oh, well. That's why it took me a while to name Biscus, 'cause it had to be right.

"Anyway," Louann continued, "anyway, that was three years ago when Biscus first showed up and me and him had fun all summer. Then, one day in the fall, Biscus didn't show up. I cried. I thought something had happened to him and then Harce told me to shut the hell up, that the stupid bird had probly flew south for the winter. I got really mad at him 'cause he called my bird stupid, but it made me happy to know that Biscus was all right."

Louann stared out into space. I had learned that it was best to keep quiet during her long pauses. If I interrupted the pause, she would lose track of her thought line. I watched as Biscus flew to the flowers, hovered around a bloom, and then flew back to Louann's shoulder. The other hummingbirds in the yard performed the same services on the flowers, but they flew to a nearby tree to rest.

"Anyway," Louann continued, "anyway, I thought about Biscus all winter that first year and then one nice day in early May, I walked out on the porch and was looking at the flowers and then sweet Biscus came flying up and set right here on my shoulder." She put her hand on her shoulder to show me. "He set right here on my shoulder like he ain't never been gone. I ast him where he'd been but he couldn't tell me and so I played like he told me he had done gone all the way to Miami and come back just to see me. We still play like he is telling me about Miami only I am asking questions and then answering them for him. Kind of like a puppet, don't you know."

She held out her hand gracefully and Biscus lit on her finger. She slowly moved her hand to her mouth and kissed him.

"Anyway," Louann continued, "anyway, this is the third year that Biscus has went away and came back again. It's like I'm his momma." She paused and looked away and continued softly, "Harce wouldn't never let me have no baby. I kind of thought a baby would have been nice. Maybe that's why I like all my animals and plants and specially Biscus so much."

I was astounded with the story. At first I thought it might be a good addition to my collection of redneck stories, but then I thought, "Aw, hell, I can't tell that story. Nobody would believe that one."

Then I looked hard at Louann. I pointed to the bruise on her face and asked, "Did you run into a door, or did Harce do that to you?"

She hung her head and softly said, "Yes, he did it. I warn't going to tell nobody."

She didn't say anything for a while. I was silent. Then she continued, "You see, John, when you and Harce quit drinking, I snuck around and drunk some beers but I was skeered he would smell it on me so I quit, too. I didn't tell nobody but I just kind of didn't drink no more. I been saving my money, too. I been able to save up a bunch not buying beer, don't you know. And, when I quit drinking, that's when Biscus started letting me kiss him. He never done that before. So I decided to stay quit just for Biscus.

"Anyway, I quit drinking and then after Harce got his leg cut off, he was hurtin' pretty bad and he took them pain pills they give him and he still hurt so he smoked him some dope and then after that, he needed more and more pain pills and he smoked more and more dope. And he started getting mean. Then he started drinking beer again and taking pain pills and he got meaner.

"And then the doctor told Harce he couldn't get no more 'scriptions for pain pills and he got really mean but he went to see Betty Sue 'cause Betty Sue is on Medicaid and she gets pain pills for free and she don't really need them so she sells them for a dollar and a half a pill. Betty Sue makes pretty good money off of that and she gives it to her boyfriend to buy gas for his motorcycle 'cause he wouldn't hang around otherwise.

"And then, Saturday night, Harce got a bunch of Sunday beer and a bunch of pills and he taken all them pills and he drunk all them beers and he kind of forgot what he was doing and passed out over there next to the barn. I taken a blanket over there and covered him up and put a tow sack under his head like a pillow.

"And then he woke up feeling kind of funny on Sunday morning and I give him a bunch of coffee but he wouldn't eat no breakfast and he seen he was out of pills and so he got Ponytail to take him over to Betty Sue's house to get him some. When he come back, he was feeling better so he went to get him some beers and they was all gone. Then he got really mean and told me that I had drunk up all them beers and I told him I hadn't touched no damn beers. And he asked me if I was calling him a liar and that was when he hit me. He didn't hit me in the face at first, but I just kind of stood there and he got madder and madder and hit me in the face and that was when I started running and he tripped on his fake leg and he just laid there on the ground yelling at me."

Tears were running down her face. Biscus hovered around and checked them out but he didn't like the taste. All I could do was watch and listen.

"And then Manuel come running up to see what all the yelling was about and when he seen what Harce had done to me he proceeded to kick Harce's ass unmerciful. And I don't know what he said to Harce 'cause it was in Mexican, but I think he was telling Harce that if he done it again he would be a dead man."

I asked, "What did Harce do?"

She looked down at the floor. "Harce cain't do nothing. He done took money from the Mexicans for the wedding and first off if the wedding don't happen, he will owe them money that he ain't got and second if he does something to Manuel, he'll be in worse trouble. Harce is skeered of them. He ain't skeered of much of nothin' but he's skeered of them."

I asked, "What would they do to him?"

She thought for a moment and said, "Well, when they give him the deposit for the wedding there was this mean looking Mexican and he told Harce that there better not nothing go wrong. Harce said that nothing wouldn't go wrong. He said he guaranteed it. And that Mexican guy just sat there and stared at Harce for a long time and it kind of gave me the willies and Harce started sweating.

"And the Mexican guy told Harce, he said, 'Harce, our business is to get people to the United States. We get some here and try to make them legal if they got enough money like Manuel does. He gives us ten thousand dollars and we give you five of it. We are giving you two thousand five hundred dollars up front to make sure everything happens. We will give you the rest when the marriage is finished. If anything happens, you will be in trouble.' And Harce asked them what kind of trouble and the mean-looking Mexican stared at him again and he said, 'I'll tell you a story. When someone just wants to get across the border, it costs them twenty five hundred dollars. They give us half of the money in Mexico, and the other half when we get them into the States. Sometimes they think they don't have to give us the other half of the money when they get here.'

"And Harce asked him what happened if they didn't have the rest of the money and the mean Mexican told him, 'Harce, do you ever now and then hear about the immigration officers finding a truck load of dead immigrants?' And Harce said yes and the mean Mexican ast him, 'Do you think that is an accident?' And Harce kind of turned white and started sweating more and told the mean Mexican that he hadn't thought about it and the mean Mexican told Harce that it would do him good to think about it because he would probly have trouble explaining how he lost his other leg."

She stood there for a long while, shaking her head slowly. Then she brightened up and said, "Thanks for the hanging baskets, John. Everybody's going to love them. I just love them hanging petunias."

I left. I had work to do. I couldn't think of any way that I could help in the situation because it was totally foreign to anything I had ever dealt with. Before leaving I had asked Louann if she needed any help or if she would report the beating to the police.

Her reply had been to slowly move Biscus to her mouth and kiss him, and then to say, "Naw, John, I don't know what is going to happen. I ain't skeered of him hitting me again with Manuel around, and I've been hit before, that ain't so bad. What I can't take, though, is the yelling."

She had repeated over and over as I walked toward the truck,
"I don't like the yelling.
I can't take the yelling.
Don't yell at me."

THE PREACHER

It will be easy to tell you about the preacher but it's going to take some doing to tell the entire wedding story. There was just so much going on.

Greg had been a friend of mine and of Harce's before I even met Harce. When Harce and I were talking about who would perform the ceremony, we both had Greg in mind and that was when we found out that we both knew him. Harce had worked on Greg's kitchen and Greg had been to my house to get flowers and to drink beer by the lake. Harce and I figured that we could do some trading either on Greg's kitchen or in his yard and that he would be happy to officiate at the ceremony.

Greg was a fly fishing fool. Before I quit drinking, he would come over for fly fishing, beer drinking, and theological discussions. I enjoyed visiting with Greg because we could have theological discussions without anyone getting angry. I always sat on the dock and watched as he gracefully sent the fly line out over the lake with its gentle S curve, landing the front-loaded floating fly line on the water. The almost-invisible leader followed and gently dropped the hand-tied lure on the surface so that it looked exactly like a water bug landing. Greg waited while he silently counted ten and then gave a small jerk to the line, making the fly sort of jump. This action was irresistible to the fish. There was a ripple as the fish checked out the fly. Greg waited patiently. He made another small jerk on the line. Then the water almost boiled as the fish came back at the fly, clearing the water as Greg pulled back on the fly rod setting the hook. He was the best fisher of fish I had ever seen.

One time I asked Greg what it was that made him so good at fly fishing. It must have been exactly the right question because he got a thoughtful look on his face and didn't say a word while he executed a perfect cast, caught a two pound bass, took it off the hook, kissed it and gently returned it to its home. He reeled in his line, set the fly rod on the dock, popped the top on a Budweiser and pulled up a chair. I saw a long afternoon coming on. Greg liked to talk almost as much as he liked to fish. That was a lot.

"Well," he started, "I was brought up in the country, in a God-fearing household. My Momma and Daddy lived in total abject fear that somehow, some way, they were going to piss off either Jesus or God or both and go to Hell. They were as good a people as they knew how to be and they were in the church every time the door was open. From the time I was born, I was in the church every time the door was open and when I got old enough, even if it weren't open, I was there to cut the grass at the church, or wash the church windows, or to do anything else that it was God's will for me to do. I don't know if that church was my second home or if it was my first home and the family house was my second home. It was a close call.

"It was a Fundamentalist Baptist church and there was plenty of singing and loud fire and brimstone preaching. I remember a bunch of times getting scared and hiding under the pew and my mother telling me that God would take care of me, but that wasn't what the preacher was saying. The preacher was saying that I was going to burn in hell just because of what I was thinking and I couldn't ever seem to control that part of me. Every time I looked at a pretty girl I thought about getting laid and I couldn't stop myself. I knew I was going to go to hell, but I couldn't stop.

"I knew that God wanted me to do good in school and so I worked hard at it. I made good grades and the church took up money and helped me get an education at a fine evangelical university. I studied hard and was ordained as a Minister of the Gospel. I met Cindy and we were chaste and pure just like we were supposed to be until we got married. Cindy had a baby boy seven months after we were married and the doctor said it was the biggest premature baby he had ever seen. I just wondered where the blonde hair and blue eyes came from. But I loved that baby and I loved Cindy and we were happy. I got a preaching job at Johnson Springs Baptist Church and the people treated me good and I loved being a preacher. I worked hard at it and I visited the halt and lame and I preached the best fire and brimstone I could muster up. I helped build the congregation from fifty people to a hundred and fifty people. I was a good preacher. I thought I was a good father and a good husband, too.

"I know I was a good preacher and a good husband and a good father. I know it in my heart. But then, one day, Cindy took the baby and ran off with one of the deacons in his Cadillac and I never saw nothing more of her but her name on the divorce papers that she filed and had me served with. Cindy wrote me a letter and told me that it wasn't anything I had done wrong but that the blonde-headed deacon was the father of the baby anyway and that she could prove it.

"She said that he was married when she got pregnant but when his wife died they decided they loved each other. That was it. I had been a good father and husband and that was gone. I was sad, but I took comfort in the fact that I was still a good preacher and that I was still a good man and a good Christian.

"Then the next blow came. Then the other five deacons that didn't run off with my wife but probably wanted to had a meeting and decided that God and Jesus and the congregation of the Johnson Springs Baptist Church didn't want a preacher who had been divorced. They told me that they were really sad and that I had done a really good job being their shepherd and that they knew that the divorce wasn't my fault. They said they would like to keep me as preacher but that the divorce made me a poor example for the congregation. Then they kicked my ass out. I was out of a job, out of an income, and I got kicked out of the parsonage which wasn't all that great, anyhow. That was when I took up fly fishing.

"I could still be a preacher if I wanted to and I still to this day have my license to marry people. I just haven't used it. I keep everything current and renewed and up to date, though, just in case, but I was fishing a trout stream one day and thought I'd be a salesman for a while. I looked around and found this job selling safety equipment and work gloves for a distributor. I got really good at it. I got to where I could put on my coat and tie and call on the executives at big companies that needed my services, or I could put on my jeans and flannel shirt and go call on the smaller companies over in Alabama. Now I'm a good salesman just like I was a good preacher. The only difference is that I make a bunch of money being a good salesman and I have time to go fly fishing. After learning what I've learned over the last few years, I might go back to preaching again someday. I don't think I will, but I might. I've thought about it."

Greg paused like he wanted some reaction so I asked, "But how does all of this make you such a good fly fisher? You're the best I've ever seen, even at tournaments."

Greg laughed. "Don't you see the connection? Look at preaching and selling and compare them to fly fishing. It all takes practice and understanding."

It was my turn to laugh. "I could probably ponder and come up with a good comparison, but I would appreciate it if you would elaborate. You've obviously thought about it more than I have."

Greg opened another Budweiser and continued, "Don't you see? It's obvious to me. Look at fly fishing: I am trying to sell a bill of goods, so I study what the fish wants to eat. I study the life forms on the lake, on the rivers, in the creeks. Then I go home and figure out how to make something that looks like what I have seen out of feathers and colored string and anything else I can find. The hard part is I have to hide a hook in it.

"Then, when I have the desired product, I have to tie my line just right. I use a tapered floating line that is bigger on the front end than the back end. This means that there is a microscopic difference gradually moving from one end to the other of a fifty foot piece of line. And that line floats. It is tapered so the weight will carry it out to where I want it. Then I fasten on a leader line that is so transparent and thin that the fish won't see it. This one is about six feet long.

The fly goes on the very end. This line goes on an eight foot fishing rod that takes me 100 hours or more to make. It is made from long tapered slivers of bamboo that I shave to perfection and glue together so that it makes an octagonal fishing rod. I tie on the eyelets and varnish and sand it with twenty thin coats. Sometimes, even after all of that, the rod doesn't work quite right and I have to start over. This one here is perfect."

He picked up the rod and showed me the action. I watched the rod move back and forth in the air as he moved it slowly. It was beautiful. Greg continued, "See, now I've got the product – that's the fly, and I have the delivery system – that's the fly rod. You might think that makes me good, but that's not all. That's just the tools. Now I have to think like a fish."

Greg got quiet and concentrated as he moved the fly rod over his head, back and forth with the same precision that a juggler might use in throwing his balls to just the perfect arc. As he moved the rod, the floating line and leader were allowed to slip from the reel as he pulled it loose and let it go. The line got out to about forty feet when he said, "Look. Watch this fly land on the water. Watch the line curl."

I watched as the line touched the water close to the dock and then curled down on the water. When the end of the floating line hit the surface, the leader curled down in the exact same manner. The fly was laid gently down on the water making a small ripple and looking exactly like a small bug lighting there.

"Now it *looks* like a bug on the water, but it doesn't *act* like a bug on the water."

He moved his arm imperceptibly and the fly kind of wiggled and moved exactly two inches. A ripple in the water indicated a bass checking it out. Greg grinned and said, "Now, one more time like this," and he moved his arm again. There was a big ripple and Greg moved the pole back and set the hook on the fish. He pulled it in, kissed it, and let it go.

"See," he said. "I had the right tools, I had the right product, but that ain't all I need. I need a perfect presentation – that's how I lay the line out there just right. I put it right in the fish's face. Right in front of him where he can't help but see how pretty it is. Then I need to convince the fish that it's really what I say it is. The final trick is to act like I'm going to take it back. I make the fish think that the bug is going to fly away and he fears a loss and goes for it. It doesn't work every time, but it gets a good percentage."

"So, in sales, the fly is the product?" I asked.

"That's right, and it has to look good and it has to at least look like it is doing what it is supposed to do."

I asked, "And after you get the potential customer's interest, you act like you will withdraw the product?"

"That's right," he said. "That's when it becomes irresistible."

I asked, "What is the product in religion?"

Greg grinned. "It's a little harder there. It could be Heaven or eternal life, it could be peace of mind, it could be a way of life. It's like tying the fly. You have to make the product for the client."

Greg paused and looked at me seriously. "Setting the hook is not always as easy as it seems, either." Then he laughed. "There are some tricks to reeling them in, too. It's not as easy as it looks. Takes practice."

"What about the kiss?" I asked.

"That's the thank you. For the fish it's a kiss and release. For the commercial customer, it's maybe a free dinner or a deep sea fishing trip or a case of liquor. It varies." He paused and thought. "For the parishioners, it can be many things, like giving them a feeling of importance, belonging, or safety. It can be many things. Sometimes a smile and a handshake will do."

Greg and I talked for a while longer. I asked him about his feelings on religion since he was no longer employed by the church.

He replied, "Once I got over my upbringing and university brainwashing and discovered that religion – not just Christianity, but religion -- was not about the *fear* of God but about the *love* of God and humanity – once I figured that out, then I could handle it."

THE WEDDING
chapter 25
PART ONE

I could smell it two miles away. By the time I got a mile closer, my mouth was watering. I thought I had an idea of what I was driving into, but looking back, I just didn't have the scale right.

It was the day of the "wedding" and I had been asked to show up early to help with any last-minute chores. I knew that this was to be the biggest event to ever occur in The Colons and I had dressed in the most appropriate manner I could muster up. My leather Birkenstocks had been spit shined, my white socks were spotless, a sharp crease had been carefully ironed in my new Levi shorts, and I had topped my outfit off with a white embroidered Cuban wedding shirt. I drove slowly and carefully. Driving through The Colons in any other manner would more than likely tear out a muffler or ruin the wheel alignment on a Sherman tank.

I turned the truck into the driveway at the sawmill and drove through a delicious cloud of smoke. I parked out of the way, backing in so that I would hopefully be able to get out at some sane hour, got out of the truck and stretched, taking in a deep breath. The smell of food was overwhelming. I took a walk to look around and see what was going on. It took some time to see it all. The scene was reminiscent of a medieval fair re-enactment.

Santos was cooking his Mexican food in one corner of the yard and was surrounded by a throng of little kids who were chasing an equal throng of Louann's chickens that had probably been let out of their pen by mistake. Manuel wore a black tuxedo and was running around chasing the children, yelling out unintelligible instructions in staccato Spanish. I walked by, laughing and shaking my head. I had heard that the Mexicans had been invited, but I didn't realize that there was going to be a cook-off. Finally, I found myself in the middle of the yard just looking around in amazement.

Louann was running around by the gazebo yelling at a bunch of rednecks who worked rapidly, following her instructions and cowering with abject fear of Louann and her big hog-chasing stick.

She yelled, "Move them tree trunks over there so we got kind of like church seats. Line them up in a half circle. I want everybody to have a seat."

The men tried to do as they were told but they couldn't quite get it right. Louann shoved a couple of them aside yelling, "Like this here! Ain't you never seen a half of a circle? Put them like this."

She man-handled the two-foot-high tree sections that Harce had cut for seats. The seating started to take the shape she liked and she headed over toward the barbecue pit to yell out more instructions. I walked in that direction.

Harce and his cronies had obviously been up all night, drinking beer and cooking three whole hogs. The hogs had been split open and stainless steel rods had been driven through the legs from one end to the other, flattening the entire presentation so that it looked like they were hung on a double cross. The hogs were laid on a metal grate that was supported by concrete blocks over a two foot deep fire pit that had been dug in the ground. The fire had been carefully prepared and burnt down to glowing coals. Ponytail and Jeffrey wore welding gloves and walked from hog to hog, picking them up by the steel rods and turning them. The hogs were almost ready and their skin was a golden brown without a burnt spot on them. Harce followed them around with a five gallon bucket of barbecue sauce which he liberally applied with a rag mop.

Louann yelled at Smitty, "Smitty, you pick up all them damn beer cans and put them in that there barrel over there. I got to go get on my wedding outfit and I don't want to come back out here and see no mess."

Louann stopped yelling for a moment, picked up a huge two pronged fork, walked over to one of the hogs, and peeled off a chunk of meat. Then, she stopped by the wood fired oven and broke off a piece of warm bread, wrapped the meat in it and brought it to me. Louann knew how to get my best performance. She smiled her Mona Lisa smile and said gently, "John, here's a taste. How 'bout if you see about getting the food laid out on the tables just right. We goin' to put the Mexican food on these tables and the barbecue and slaw over there. You kin get anybody you want to help you. Just tell them if they don't do right Louann is gon' to whip them. They better mind." She disappeared.

I thought I'd better take inventory before supervising the placement of food, so I walked over to check out the Mexican territory. Santos had a fifty-five gallon barrel stood up on end with a fire in it. He was proud of his barrel. He showed me where Harce had cut holes and made vents so that he could regulate the fire. A large, tapered, stainless steel pot sat partly in and partly out of the top of the barrel. Santos had started with the white fat from inside a hog and had cooked it down into clear lard. He had added pork skins which he called "chicharones" and cooked up a large bowl full of fried pork skins.

I tried a piece and decided that he had taken fried pork skins to another dimension. About twenty or thirty pounds of meat cut into four inch squares had been dumped into the oil and Santos was stirring them with a boat paddle. He called this "carnitas." Santos stood there grinning with smoke framing his plump face, stirring with his boat paddle. He looked up at me, "Hey, Juan. Lookee new barrel. Like it new barrel."

I looked around some more. Antonia had prepared about twenty gallons of fajita mix with beef, chicken, and pork strips. She stood in front of a charcoal grill with a piece of flat steel on top of it and was simultaneously supervising two Mexican ladies, who were patting hand made tortillas between their hands, and making quesadillas. Antonia laid a tortilla on the hot flat steel and then piled on strips of chicken, onions, peppers, and grated white cheese, covering half of the tortilla. Next she folded the other half of the tortilla over the meat and cheese, pressed it down with a spatula, and turned the ten or more prepared quesadillas one at the time so that they were cooked to a golden brown. She piled them on a large wooden platter off to one side. Little Gabriella stood by the food with a fan, chasing away the flies.

Santos finished with the carnitas and began loading corn tortillas that had been cut into triangles into the oil. He watched them carefully, pulling them out when they were perfectly golden brown. "Taco chips," he said with a smile as he piled them on several layers of newspaper to drain. "Taco chips – perfecto." Then he rattled off some Spanish to Rosaria who was preparing gallons of what looked to be searing hot salsa. I took out my pad and made notes on what needed to go where.

Back in the redneck-cooking territory, Harce and Ponytail had started pulling the meat from the hogs and Marsha and Misty were finishing up the slaw and baked beans. I passed out large pieces of aluminum foil to cover all of the plates and serving pans and gave out instructions on where everything should go. The women, of course, both Mexican and redneck, modified my instructions, so I walked off knowing that all would be performed satisfactorily.

While I had been checking out the food, cars had been showing up. Lots of cars. Lots of trucks. Most of Harce and Louann's friends drove pick-up trucks and as they showed up, the men went to the edge of the woods and set up tents. They knew they weren't going to drive home that night. The Mexicans seemed to prefer smaller cars—especially small Hondas. I could see sleeping bags in the back windows. I guess no tents were needed.

Soon there was a crowd. Mexicans gathered around Santos' barrel, admiring it, and the rednecks wandered around checking out the flower covered gazebo and the barbecue. Everyone but me and a few of the women held a beer can. It was noisy and fun. The redneck kids had begun chasing chickens with the Mexican kids. They were yelling and laughing in two languages and I smiled because it seemed that language difficulties made absolutely no difference to children.

Manuel had disappeared.

Greg, the preacher, showed up in his Mercedes, parking very carefully with an exit strategy in mind. He had brought his friend Ginger to be Matron of Honor because he accurately guessed that Louann would have missed out on that detail. Greg was dressed in a dark blue Armani suit with gleaming shoes, a white shirt and a red tie tied in a four in hand. Ginger was wearing a garden hat with a floppy brim, which bobbed with every step. The hat was white, with a large red rose attached to the front of the brim. Her dress was white chiffon with black polka dots, clinging to her ample bosom and gracefully flowing from her thighs. Her high heels were red with a matching pocketbook over one arm, a nosegay of red roses and lilies of the valley in the other hand. Ginger had brought a pile of hand-made sugar mints of different colors nested in rose petals on a silver tray.

Lindsey drove carefully into the driveway in his perfectly restored white '65 fastback Mustang. He paused to study the parking situation, backed his car in and proceeded to unload his amp and his antique Martin guitar. Lindsey grinned at me and I got a couple of rednecks to help him with his musical paraphernalia.

I had been asked to arrange for a singer for the wedding and Lindsey was the best at this that I knew. He loved to sing at such affairs. His music was different from what the guests were used to, but I knew they would like it.

I looked around for Kickstand and Bud, but I didn't see them. I thought that was kind of funny. I soon found out how funny it was.

I thought I heard thunder. I muttered to myself, "Aw, man, that's just what we need here is a big rain storm." But I looked at the sky and saw nothing but blue. The noise was steady—not intermittent like thunder – and it seemed to grow in intensity. The rumbling got louder and louder and seemed to come from all around but mostly from the end of the road leading to Harce's house. Every one at the gathering stopped what they were doing and stared as a multitude of Harley Davidson motorcycles turned the corner heading slowly up the dirt road toward the driveway. There must have been fifty or more Harleys in a convoy. Leading the pack on immaculately cleaned and polished motorcycles were Bud and Kickstand with big grins on their faces.

The bikers were mostly dressed in leathers or jeans and tank tops. Most of the men had a woman riding behind with leather pants and short shirts that showed their tattoos. I noticed a yellow dot in the center of each headlight.

The bikers pulled into the pasture on the other side of the fence behind the Mexican cooks. They parked in a formation, dismounted and started pulling the stickers from their headlights and moving toward Kickstand who had a clip board and a set of measuring calipers. There was a lot of jovial argument and yelling as the stickers were carefully measured to determine which one had a bug closest to the center. Candyman busied himself removing the bungee cords which secured a large trophy to the back of his bike. He finally held the trophy over his head and carried it over to Kickstand's "command station." Bud stood nearby counting a large handful of cash.

The bikers milled around noisily, checking the measuring progress and finally there was a big yell as Kickstand proclaimed, "The winner is Broom Sage. His bug is dead center. I hereby proclaim him the winner of the Bug Run Championship." Broom Sage approached the command station proudly, strutting up and showing off his polished leather pants and making muscles with his tattooed arms. The trophy was the most important award of the year. There was applause and back slapping. Broom Sage jumped up and down yelling, holding the trophy up over his head. Cans of Budweiser were passed out all around and all the bikers gathered in a loose circle, toasting. "Here's to Louann!" yelled Kickstand. "This is her day. Let's Party!!"

Bud had climbed up on a picnic table and was looking out over the crowd. He spotted me, caught my eye, and gestured for me to wait for him. He jumped down from his perch and made his way through the crowd to where I stood. He held the cash tightly in one hand and a manila envelope in the other. He grinned at me. "Hey, John, tell your preacher friend that we need to make an announcement at the end of the wedding. We done set up this here Bug Run for Louann 'cause everybody likes her so much and we got to give her something before everybody gets too drunk to notice. Now, don't you say nothing to nobody but the preacher, y'hear?" I promised and went off to find

Greg.

I found Greg, Ginger, and Lindsey in the gazebo. Greg was talking with Lindsey about the music while Ginger was trying to communicate with Manuel and his two brothers with sign language and slow English. I guess she thought that if she spoke loudly and slowly they would understand her. It was kind of funny to watch. Manuel was attired in a black tuxedo with a red cummerbund and his two brothers wore white tuxedoes with black cummerbunds. They were really trying to understand and had looks of concentrations on their faces as Ginger pointed and moved them from place to place, getting everything just right. I spoke briefly with Greg and he nodded affirmation just as Harce started vigorously ringing the large dinner bell.

The crowd had gathered around the gazebo, sitting on stumps, standing, and sitting on the ground. Lindsey turned up the amp and began playing a jazzed-up, four-fingered picking rendition of *The Wedding March* on his Martin guitar. Everyone in the crowd got silent and turned toward the house as the door slowly opened and Louann, April, and Maybell appeared on the porch.

All the audience could do was stare.

chapter 26 THE WEDDING: PART TWO

April and Maybell were the bridesmaids. They walked out slowly wearing tight red short shorts with sleeveless wraparound blouses in a summer swirl print, their feet wobbling slightly in bright red spike-heeled shoes. They paused as April took one last long drag on her Marlboro Light, bent over, and stubbed it out on a stepping stone. I chuckled as I listened to the spontaneous male sigh when she bent over. It was quite a sight.

Everyone drew a deep breath in admiration as Louann stepped out on the porch with her Mona Lisa smile. She stood there looking over the crowd, taking in the sight. Then she stooped to pick up April's cigarette butt and placed it in an ash can by the door. She was wearing a satin ensemble consisting of tight white short shorts and a matching short sleeve shirt on which she had meticulously painted a red hibiscus bloom over the left breast and a hovering hummingbird over the right one. Her shirt sleeve covered most of the bruise on her right arm. She wore a wide brimmed straw hat with one red rose off to the left side. Louann's feet were bare. Her beautiful, sexy toes had been painted to perfection with red nail polish. Three small diamonds had been imbedded in the nails of her big toes. Well, anyway, they did look like diamonds. I'm not sure.

I glanced sideways to where Harce stood. He had a strange,

confused look on his face. Harce was standing beside the Mexican organizer who was there to make sure the wedding went off as planned. I assumed that the bulge in his pocket was the rest of the money that Harce was to receive. I decided to ignore them.

The ceremony itself went well. Greg, of course, had no idea that the wedding was set up to make Manuel legal, so he performed a very traditional ceremony. He started out with, "Dearly beloved, we are gathered here," and proceeded from there. There were actually no problems until he asked, "Manuel, do you take this woman, Louann, to be your lawfully wedded wife," at which time Manuel turned to his brother who spoke a little English. The brother rattled out a little Spanish, and Manuel turned to the preacher and said, "Si." Then he paused and continued haltingly, "Yes, I do."

Greg turned to Louann. "Do you take this man, Manuel, to be your lawfully wedded husband?" Louann looked down at her feet for a long while, studying the pattern of diamonds on her toes. She looked up at Manuel. She gazed back to where Harce was standing. Then she looked back at the preacher, held her head up high, and, in a loud, clear voice, she said, "I do." And when Greg said, "You may kiss the bride," Manuel got a confused look on his face as Louann grabbed him and kissed him long and hard. She pressed her entire body against him and kissed him like he had probably never been kissed before. All I could see of Manuel's face were his eyebrows which were raised high in surprise. He did, however, seem to enjoy the kiss.

The couple held hands and turned to face the diverse congregation. Manuel was very serious and Louann resumed her Mona Lisa smile as Lindsey sang what he had told me was his favorite love song which had been written in England by Dr. Ben Jonson and later passed down to Lindsey by his Tennessee ancestors. The crowd was totally silent as his beautiful tenor voice rang out over the farm.

> *Drink to me only with thine eyes,*
> *And I will pledge with mine;*
> *Or leave a kiss but in the cup,*
> *And I'll not look for wine.*
> *The thirst, that from the soul doth rise,*

Doth ask a drink divine:
But might I of Jove's nectar sup,
I would not change for thine.

I sent thee, late, a rosy wreath,
Not so much honoring thee,
As giving it a hope, that there
It could not withered be.
But thou thereon did'st only breathe,
And sent'st it back to me:
Since when it grows, and smells, I swear,
Not of itself, but thee.

Lindsey finished singing and looked down at his guitar for a moment. Then he looked out over the crowd and grinned, his white teeth showing through his grey beard. There was a dead silence in the audience. I saw tears in some of the women's eyes. Louann had listened to the song with total concentration and when it was over, she stared at Lindsey for a long moment and then turned to look Manuel in the face. I could see her squeeze his hand. I turned to look at Harce just in time to see the big, mean Mexican hand him a handful of cash and walk off.

Then Greg took charge and said in his loud baritone voice, "If you will remain, Kickstand and Bud have an important announcement to make. Bud, Kickstand, come on up here."

Bud and Kickstand walked up to the gazebo, picking their way through the crowd. Kickstand looked a little self-conscious in front of so many people, but he took Lindsey's microphone and began his talk.

"Folks, I know everybody here who knows Louann knows how special she is to all of us. They ain't a one of us who ain't enjoyed her Brunswick stew or ate her wonderful blackberry jelly. She has took care of us when we needed her to and she has always been around to comfort us when our girlfriends run off or when our coon dogs died." He paused. "'Specially when our coon dogs died." There was a big chuckle from the crowd. Kickstand paused like a seasoned performer.

"Anyway, since Louann has been so good to us, we done had a Bug Run just for today. We decided that the winner would get a trophy instead of money and that all of the money would go to this here gift certificate that I'm holding." He held up a piece of paper. "Bud, here is gon to read it to you as I ain't too good at that."

Bud stepped up to the mike, took the paper and grinned out over the audience. He was in his element and not afraid of anything – not even public speaking. He got everyone's attention and began. "We almost had a war over what to do for Louann, and then we started talking about how she was always smiling when she meant to be grinning. That's how we come up with this here idea for a present." He paused, looked down at the paper, and started reading. "This here is a gift certificate for Louann in that we have worked it out with Doctor Shapiro that the proceeds of this here Bug Run is to pay for Doctor Shapiro to fix her teeth so she can grin instead of always having that little smile she always has 'cause she is afraid to grin 'cause she don't like the way her teeth look. And we done told Doctor Shapiro that if it ain't enough we will make another Bug Run and give him some more money and that Louann is got to give Doctor Shapiro one jar of blackberry jam and two quarts of Brunswick stew for her part."

There was a stunned silence in the audience. Louann dropped her head and started crying. Then she hugged Bud and Kickstand really big. Lindsey started playing some kind of classical music on the guitar that I didn't recognize, and everybody walked out of the gazebo and out of the yard over to the food tables and the beer coolers.

Harce and his welding buddies had made a cannon that they loaded with welding oxygen and then set off with a match. They fired it until the barrel got red hot. People sat everywhere eating – on the ground, on the porch, on the stumps, and in the grass. I had never seen food and beer disappear so rapidly. Lindsey had put a country music mix on the amplifier and turned it way up. Every once in a while he put on some Mexican music. An area was cleared in front of the gazebo for dancing. That's when the cultures mixed. The rednecks danced a clog to fiddle music while the Mexicans performed their wild hip-gyrating sexual moves. Both cultures seemed to fit together on the "dance floor." Members of both groups danced, took breaks to eat and drink, and then danced some more. After a while, one of Manuel's brothers rang the dinner bell and everyone stopped to see what was going on.

I looked up at the gazebo and saw that while no one was looking, Lindsey and three or four Mexicans had set up a combo. There were drums, a bass guitar, a keyboard, and Lindsey playing his guitar. Lindsey was good enough to play anything with anybody and was checking out chords and progressions with the Mexican musicians while everyone tuned up.

I had been to a couple of Mexican weddings before, and I thought I knew what was coming. The Mexicans are conscious of money or the lack thereof and they never want anyone to be publicly embarrassed over not having much so they have developed a process for bestowing wedding presents on the bride that allows a bit of anonymity. The rednecks watched curiously while one of Manuel's brothers passed out straight pins to all of the men. The band started up a slow dancing tune with a repetitious melody. It was a song that could go on and on for a long time.

The "dance floor" was cleared and Manuel took Louann by the hand and led her to the center of it. Everyone gathered in a large circle around the dancing area and clapped hands in time to the music while the newly married couple danced for a few minutes.

When the dancing couple had danced around to all parts of the circle, Manuel's brother came out to tap Manuel on the shoulder. Manuel relinquished his bride and the brother danced her around the circle. While they danced, he used the straight pin to fasten a ten dollar bill to the back of her blouse. At this point, another Mexican moved into the circle to dance with Louann and Manuel and the brother caught up a couple of biker chicks to dance with. As the band repeated the music over and over, one person after another came up to dance with Louann and pin a bill of one denomination or another on her blouse. The rednecks eventually caught on and approved of the practice, forming a line to dance with the bride and pin money to her shirt. After a while, there was no more room on her shirt and the bikers took over, pinning bills to bills so that long strings of ones, tens and twenties cascaded around her. Greg danced for a moment and with a large grin on his face, pinned a hundred dollar bill right over the hummingbird. As each dancer left the bride with her gift, they chose a partner to dance with and the dancing area slowly filled to capacity and was stretched farther and farther into the pasture. The band played on until everyone sober enough to walk was dancing. There was laughter and trading off of partners. Even the children started to dance, not caring if they could speak the same language or not. It was quite a sight.

The band started mixing American country music with the Mexican music. People danced who had never even thought of dancing before. It was contagious. People would dance, take a break for more food and beer, and go back to dancing again. The chickens got loose and started running around underfoot, getting stepped on and squawking and flapping their wings. I was just glad that the dogs had been securely tied up. When it got dark, Harce and his friends built a bonfire of lumber scraps to light up the night. The dancing went on and on until many of the guests retired to their tents in the woods, either exhausted or drunk or both.

I went for a walk around the property. The mess wasn't as big as I had thought it would be because the guests had been careful to put paper plates and beer cans in the proper containers. I still made a mental note to be scarce the next day when the clean up took place. When I looked in the dog pen, I found that so many meat scraps had been tossed to the dogs that they just sat and stared at the meat, not being able to eat another bite. A lot of the guests were in the same shape.

I decided that it was time for me to go and went all over the place looking for Manuel and Louann to say good bye, but I guessed they were lost somewhere in the crowd. I spoke with Lindsey and thanked him for his help with the music. I traded a few words with Bud and Kickstand, telling them how much I admired what they did with the Bug Run and how much it seemed to mean to Louann. I found Santos and Antonia and told them how good the food was. I had almost killed myself with the quesadillas. I went to find Harce.

I found Harce sitting on a stump in front of the gazebo with a can of beer in one hand, a cigarette in the other hand, and a glazed look on his face. It was a glazed look that was caused by more than beer. He looked up at me. "John, John? Is that you?" He took a big swallow of beer. "I cain't find Louann," he said. "I'm looking for her 'cause it's time for her to rub oil on this here leg stump. I cain't find her nowhere."

I told him that I hadn't seen Louann, either and that she was probably lost in the crowd somewhere. Harce kind of nodded. His head fell down on his chest and let out a sound that was somewhere between a moan and a snore. He looked up at me and said, "I hope she ain't done run off with her husband."

His head fell back down on his chest as he passed out.

chapter 27
EGG ROLLS

"Hey, Bud, do you smell egg rolls?"

Bud got a funny smile on his face. "I'll bet Kickstand will be here in a minute."

"How do you know that?" I asked.

"You'll see."

It was an early Saturday morning, a week after the wedding, and Bud and I had been drinking coffee on the dock at the lake, trying not to catch any fish. He watched his red and white bobber while I pulled in an empty fly line. We had run a drop cord to the dock to power the coffee maker. I heard what sounded like a rather loud diesel engine approach the driveway and start up the hill. The smell of Chinese egg rolls permeated the morning air. I set the fly rod down on the dock, took a sip of coffee, and turned to see what was coming. I never knew what was going to happen on a Saturday morning at the lake, and I surely wasn't ready for what I saw.

The vehicle pulled around the corner. It was painted burnt orange and cream. The paint job was perfect and shiny. The front of the "car" was obviously from an older Mercedes diesel sedan. It had been modified, however, with the back seat cut out and the rear end turned into what looked like the bed of a pick up truck. It looked good enough to be on the showroom floor. I walked over to investigate and saw two fifty-five gallon drums sitting in the bed with copper pipes carefully wrapped around them. I stood looking in wonder as the driver's side door opened and Kickstand climbed out with a big grin on his face.

I walked around the car/truck, checking out all of the perfectly cut and finished welds. It was amazing. Kickstand had that look on his face that a small boy gets when he is showing off something special. "How do you like my new 'cruck?'"

I shook my head and grinned. "I guess you'd better tell me about it, Kickstand."

"Well, it all started when gas prices went up so high. I had been laid off between shutdowns and I didn't have nothing to do and I had a bunch of time and money on my hands. That's when I got to studying different ways to make something run. Then I got this old '79 Mercedes diesel and started fooling with it." He took a rag out of his pocket and gently wiped a bit of dust from the grill.

"You see, Adolph Diesel invented this motor a long time ago back when Henry Ford was working on starting up an assembly line. Diesel made it to run off of corn oil and soybean oil and stuff like that. Old Henry wanted to use the diesel engine, but the oil people got involved and all kind of stuff happened and Henry struck a deal to make cars that used gasoline instead so the oil people could get rich. That's where all the problems in the world come from. It's all about oil and now we got to spend all our money to buy gas."

Bud said, "I've done heered about it, but I ain't seen it." He walked over and raised the hood. There was a motor with funny tubes and wires running all over. The motor was clean and polished. Bud ran his hands lovingly over the motor, grinning with the admiration that a seasoned mechanic has for a clean motor.

Kickstand explained, "I figured out that I could switch this here motor over and run it off of vegetable oil if I did it right. Then, I found out that I could get almost free vegetable oil from the fast food restaurants after they had throwed it away after they cooked their French fries and stuff."

Kickstand became animated. He waved his arms and pointed as he continued, "I played with straining the used vegetable oil and cleaning it up. I got me a five-foot piece of four-inch pvc pipe and I took me some duck tape and put some of the old lady's panty hose over the bottom end of it and strained that oil through it. Then I looked at it and strained it some more. I strained it thirteen times until it was clear and clean and I could see through it. I made sure it would burn clean and then I started changing the injectors around and fooled with the oil and the injectors until I could squirt them into a mason jar and the spray made a perfect cone. I put it all together and then I used a little bit of diesel fuel to start the motor and then switched over to the vegetable oil."

Kickstand looked me in the eye and raised his eyebrows. "Then the sumbitch worked. You could of knocked me over with a feather."

He walked to the back of the cruck. "Here's where I keep the oil, in these barrels. I got a separate fuel pump so I can switch it back and forth. To start with, I took off the lid of the trunk and put the barrels there, but that didn't look good, so I took my cutting torch and cut out the back seat to make it look like a pick up truck. Then one thing led to another and I cut and welded and sanded and made it look like a real pick up truck. I couldn't think of nothing else but this cruck and so to finish it off, I painted it with twelve coats of hand-rubbed lacquer."

He ran his hands lovingly over the carefully painted hood. "You know how it is. You get into something and you can't stop 'til it's perfect."

I looked at Bud. He was beside himself, checking out all of the hookups and modifications. He pointed to the copper tubing running around the barrels. "What's these here copper pipes for?"

Kickstand showed Bud where the pipes went. "See, the first thing I learnt was that the vegetable oil got a little thicker on a cold morning and it wouldn't work right, so I got an idea from Grandpa's old still and I hooked these tubes up to the radiator. I can start the engine on diesel and heat it up and then the hot water from the radiator warms up the oil and I can switch it over and it works just fine." He paused. "And, I ain't got no trouble finding this here cruck in a parking lot, neither."

Bud was beside himself. "How much does it cost to run this here cruck?"

Kickstand grinned really large. "I drove it to Chattanooga and back. It costed me forty-two cents, but that ain't the good part. The good part is that I get to screw the oil people."

That was when I looked over at Bud's fishing pole. He had left the baited hook and bobber in the lake and something was pulling his fishing pole toward the edge of the dock. He ran over and grabbed the pole just as it was going over the side of the dock and started reeling in a fish. Kickstand and I walked over to watch as Bud pulled in a two pound bass, took it off the hook, kissed it, and gently put it back in the water. He set his pole down, poured three cups of coffee, and sat in a lawn chair. Kickstand and I picked up our cups and joined him. I halfway expected Kickstand to start rolling a joint, and I was surprised when he just sipped his coffee and leaned back. Kickstand must have known what I was thinking because he looked at me and said. "There ain't no pot to be found around here no more. They had this big bust in Atlanta and the cops have been really coming down on it. Everybody I know has been doing something different, but I don't want no part of it. I guess I'll just do without."

We sat and sipped coffee in silence for a while. Finally, Bud looked up and asked. "You seen Harce?"

Kickstand slowly lit a cigarette, blew out the smoke and shook his head sadly. "I went to show him my cruck last night and he was sitting there in the gazebo and he was wasted on beer and pain pills. He's mad and he's sad, and he don't know what to do since Louann done run off with her husband. He cain't find her and I think he's done got hooked on them pain pills that he was taking when they cut off his leg. I taken him a Whopper and some French fries 'cause he ain't eating much, and there was a big stack of beer cans all around him. He was mean, too. I was skeered to stay around too long, so I left." He sipped coffee and smoked. "I went to see Sobrina, too, to see if she had any pot to sell, but she said there warn't none and she was thinking about starting to make this new stuff that I told you I heard about in Tennessee. It's called meth. I just don't know about that stuff. People I've talked to says it makes you feel real good and that you can work

all day, but I just don't know. People I've seen that tried it cain't seem
to get enough of it and it makes them act weird. I think after they've
done it a while, they get pictures in their head. What do you call that,
John?"

"Hallucinations?"

"Yeah, that's it. Hallucinations. And they get all jittery and they
just don't look good. I got some good friends doing that stuff and I
guess I'm kind of worried about them. That stuff is cheap, too, and
Sobrina told me I could make it in my bathtub, but I decided if I'm
going to make anything, I'll just stick with my vegetable oil."

Bud asked, "What are we going to do about Harce?"

Kickstand put out his cigarette and drained his coffee cup. "I jest
don't know, Bud. Them pain pills and beer makes him mean, and you
don't want to be around him when he's mean 'cause he's likely to take
a axe handle to you. He keeps talking about how Louann wouldn't of
left him if he hadn't done lost his leg and he don't understand that
she wouldn't of left him if he had treated her better and not made her
get him beers and yell at her and beat on her. I don't think she's ever
gon come back 'cause she's skeered of him and 'cause he's done treated
her so bad. Anyhow, he just sits there and stares out into the woods
and if you say anything to him he gets mad and starts yelling at you.
I just don't know what to do. I don't know if there's anything we can
do."

The three of us sat there in silence for a while. I guess each of
us was lost in his own thoughts – most of them about Harce. Finally,
Kickstand stood up and said, "I got to go. I got to be at my new job by
lunch time."

I glanced up. "New job?"

Kickstand started walking over toward his cruck. "Yeah, I'm doing
pretty good. See, it happened like this. I started out running my cruck
on oil I got from the Burger King, and it did good, so I started trying
out different places to get used oil from. The Burger King oil smelled
like French fries when I burned it and then I tried oil from Sonny's
barbecue and then one day I stopped at the Golden Panda Palace and
got some used oil from them. It worked a lot better than any of the
other oil. I don't know if it is a different kind of oil, or if they just cook

it hotter and that makes a difference. Anyhow, Mister Lee, who runs the restaurant, found out what I was using it for and wanted me to pay him for it and I didn't want to give him no money, so we made a deal that since it didn't cost me much of nothing to run the cruck and he needed somebody to deliver for him, I would deliver some Chinese food now and then to pay him. I get to keep the tips, so it comes out good. I didn't have nothing better to do, anyhow."

Bud and I followed Kickstand as he walked over to his cruck. He reached into the passenger side window, pulled out a couple of magnetized signs, and placed them gently on the outside of the doors, adjusting them so that they were centered and level.

"It's turned into a pretty good job. You see, the oil from the Golden Panda Palace restaurant makes the exhaust smell like egg rolls. Someone will call in for a delivery and I'll take it to one of them rich folk's neighborhoods and make a delivery. Then, when I get back, everybody in the whole neighborhood will of seen the truck and smelt the egg rolls and the phone will be ringing. All them people living around where I made the first delivery done smelt my cruck and got hungry for Chinese food and they seen the sign, and called and ordered food for themselves. It's funny how it works. And it don't cost nothing for me to deliver and I get the tips and Mr. Lee gives me the vegetable oil and slides me some money now and then. He's happy and I'm happy and the customers are happy."

Kickstand paused and thought for a moment. "You know, if I'm happy and you're happy, and everybody else is happy, then ain't nobody got no problems."

Kickstand got in his cruck, started up the diesel engine, and drove off, leaving a cloud of egg roll scented smoke. Bud and I watched him as he turned out on the main road. Bud said, "Damn, John, I'm all of a sudden starved to death. How much does that Chinese food cost?"

chapter 28
TITLE PAWN

"H-h-h-ey, J-john, H-h-h harce needs a f-f-f-favor."

"Why doesn't he ask for it himself?"

We were standing outside my front door on a Saturday morning. I had invited him in, but for some reason, Ponytail would never enter the house. He looked at the ground. "I-I-I t-t- think he's kindly e-e-embarrassed to ast you, but he nnnneeds to b-b-b-borry your ch-ch-chain saw."

I was shocked. "Borrow my chain saw?" I asked. "Ponytail, you know as well as I do that a man doesn't loan out his chain saw. Loaning out a chain saw is like letting someone go to bed with your wife." I was right, too. Chain saws, pickup trucks and women were not to be shared. I thought everybody knew that. I knew that Harce and Ponytail knew it.

Ponytail never looked up. "Well, s-s-s-see, he's g-g-g-got to cut up some wwwwood to make some money and his ch-ch-ch-chain saw is in the hock shop, and he c-c-c-cain't get it out without he cc-c-c-cuts some wood and m-m-makes some money and he c-c-c-c-cain't cut some w-wood without no ch-ch-ch-chain saw."

"He pawned his chain saw?" I paused, trying to understand. "Why in the world would he pawn his chain saw?"

"He n-n-n-needed some m-m-money bad."

"What did he need money bad enough for to pawn his chain saw?"

"I c-c-c-c-cain't t-t-tt-tell you."

"Well, you go get Harce and bring him here and tell him we'll talk about it. I'll help him out, but I won't do it through you."

Ponytail never looked up from the ground. "I done t-t-t-t-tole him th-th-th-that you wwwwould say s-s-something like that." He shook his head and his ponytail flopped over his shoulder. "I done t-t-t-tole him to c-c-c-c-come with me, bb-b-b-but he didn't want to and I had t-t-t-t-to do what he s-said 'cause I got a pp-p-p-problem, too and he won't he'p me unless I g-g-g-get the ch-ch-ch-chain saw."

I was in a quandary. It was definitely against the rules to hand over my chain saw, but if Harce and Ponytail needed help, I needed to see what I could do. I knew that if I loaned it to him he would keep on borrowing it. It was kind of a "teach a man to fish" situation. I thought long and hard about it. "You go get Harce and tell him we'll work it out." I paused and thought. "Has he been drinking today?"

Ponytail looked at me with a funny, evasive expression. "N-n-n-naw, he ain't been drinking t-t-t-ttoday." He turned and headed toward his truck. "I'll g-g-gg-go get him."

After Ponytail left, I decided that since it was an early Saturday morning, I would sit on the dock and drink some coffee. I did three of my favorite things: I grabbed a Mark Twain book – I think it was *Innocents Abroad*, -- I put on a John Prine tape, and I grabbed a cup of coffee. I read about Twain's adventures in Venice while Prine sang:

Blow up the TV
Throw away the papers
Move to the country, build you a home
Plant a little garden
Eat a lot of peaches
Try to find Jesus
On your own.

I was lost in my reverie, my reading, and the beautiful morning when Ponytail and Harce showed up to interrupt it. Harce was doing good with his new leg but he looked as if he had lost some weight. He looked sad.

I jumped right in on him. "Harce, what's this about you taking your chain saw to the pawn shop?"

"Well, I needed some money and I hocked it. I been paying on it every week."

"How much did you get for it?" I asked. "That's a five hundred dollar Husquevarner."

"Well, I got a hunnert and sixty four dollars for it. I been paying twenty five dollars a week on it and I went yesterday afternoon to make the last payment and the sumbitch tole me that I still owe a hunnert dollars and I done showed him that I paid him all the money with ten dollars to spare and he done tole me that most of all I paid was interest." He poured a cup of coffee. "I cain't get it out without I go cut some wood and I cain't cut some wood without a saw and I knowed I could probly use yours." He looked at me without looking me in the eye. "I just don't understand how that pawn shop stuff works, but I ain't never gon' do it again."

This was a pondering situation, so I took a few moments. "Harce, I thought about it and winter is coming on and I need some firewood. There's a big oak tree down up behind the greenhouse. Why don't you and Ponytail use my saw and cut it up to firewood lengths and split and stack it. After that, I'll go get your chain saw out of the pawn shop for you. I've been saving up the money I would have spent on beer and a load of firewood would be a nice thing to have."

I must have said the right thing because Harce brightened. "You gon' go get the saw while we cut wood?"

"No, I'm going to help you cut wood and then we will go together to get the saw. Let's go to work."

Harce didn't say anything else. He headed toward the barn yelling, "I'll get the saw. Ponytail, you get the 'godevil' and we gon' take care of this here situation."

Ponytail had a look on his face that told me his day was in the process of being ruined. He went to the barn and picked up the wood-splitting tool known as a 'godevil,' which looks like a long handled sledge hammer only one side of the head is shaped like an axe and the other side is shaped like a hammer head. The rednecks call it a godevil because they say, "You pick it up and you go like the devil."

I always knew Harce could work hard, but I never saw anybody work that hard before or since. He was like a man possessed. He ran the saw wide open, cutting the limbs from the tree trunk first and then starting on the four foot thick trunk. He would cut a while and then stand the pieces up on end for Ponytail to split them with the godevil. My job was to stack the wood as it got split and I had trouble keeping up. Every now and then, Harce would take the godevil from Ponytail and start swinging it. Every time he hit a piece of wood with the godevil it was in just the right place and the wood split with a single swing. A job that would have taken a normal man a day and a half or two days was accomplished in a little over four hours. Harce wouldn't even stop to eat lunch. He made his final cuts, took the splitter from Ponytail, and split the remaining three pieces of tree trunk. He grabbed the saw and the godevil, walked over to put them in the barn and said, "Ok. Let's go get my damn chain saw."

I followed Ponytail and Harce to the pawn shop. For some reason, Harce didn't want to ride with me. He had been distant all day and had never once looked me in the eye. I sort of figured he was embarrassed about the saw, but I found out the real reason much later. We parked, and I followed them into the shop. Harce's fake foot made quite a racket on the old wooden floor as he stomped up to face the man behind the counter. "This here's John, and we come to get my chain saw out of here." I just stood there, looking around in amazement at the array of tools, electronics, guitars, and all sorts of other items. All of them had price tags attached.

I pulled a hundred dollar bill out of my pocket and laid it on the counter while the attendant went to the back room to get the saw. He put it on the counter next to my money, examined the ticket that was wired to the saw handle and said, "That will be a hundred and twelve dollars and fourteen cents."

Harce became livid and shouted, "You told me the day before yesterday it would be a hunnert dollars."

The attendant looked at him. "That was the day before yesterday. Interest keeps going on." Ponytail looked concerned and moved between Harce and the counter, obviously sensing some impending violence.

I reached in my pocket and pulled out a ten and a five. "Here, then, maybe this will settle it up if there hasn't been any more interest added since we came into the store."

A little bit of paper work was done, Harce took the saw and we walked out into the parking lot. He put the saw in the back of Ponytail's truck and turned to shake my hand.

"Thanks," he said. "Now I ain't got to worry about that no more. But we didn't get no chance to talk today. You got any more of that coffee at the house?" I thought I noticed a slight shakiness when he shook my hand.

I was rather tired from the day's work, but Harce was right, we hadn't had a chance to talk so we drove back to the house, made a pot of coffee, and went to sit on the dock. I led off the conversation. "So, Harce, how have things been going? I haven't seen you in a month."

Harce sipped his coffee. "I guess I ain't been doing too well since Louann run off with her husband. I been keeping the animals fed and such as that but the flars ain't looking too good 'cause I ain't been watering them. I just kind of sit in the gazebo and look out into the woods. I cain't seem to get much of nothing done." He stopped and stared off over the lake like he was looking at the other side of the universe. "I just don't seem to want to do nothing."

"Are you still taking those pain pills?" I asked

"I got to have them pills," he said. "And I drink some beer in the evenings when I got enough money to buy some." He stared off again for a long time. He put his elbows on his knees and his head in his hands. "I JUST GET SO LONESOME!" He sat there like that for some time. No one said a word.

Something else from the morning had been in the back of my head for a while and during the silence, I figured out what it was. I turned to Ponytail. "Didn't you tell me this morning that you had a problem, too?"

Ponytail had been lost in thought also and he looked up and said, "Yeah, I do have a pp-p-p-problem. T-t-t-t-title p-p-pawn."

I had seen signs at car lots here and there that said "title pawn," but I didn't really know what that meant. "What's 'title pawn' mean?" I asked.

Ponytail looked me straight in the eye. "Th-th-that means that when you n-n-n-n-need some money, yyyyyou take them the t-t-t-t-title to your t-t-t-t-truck and they gg-g-give you some money and you p-pay it back so much a mmmonth or so much a wwweek or whatever. It's k-k-k-kind of like a pawn shop but for c-c-c-cars."

"Did you pawn the title to your truck?"

"Yeah, I d-d-d-did that about eight months ago and they gg-g-g-g-give me eight hunnert d-d-d-d-dollars and I been pppaying them back a hunnert d-d-d-dollars a month. But they t-t-t-t-told me that only went for the interest and I ssstill owe them eight h-h-h-h-hunnert dollars and if I don't keep paying them, they send a repo man with a wrecker t-t-t-t-truck out to get my pppickup."

Now I knew what "title pawn" meant. I guess that's how they got the cars for their car lots. I thought about it for a minute. "Does anyone owe you any money, Ponytail?"

"Jest Harce, and he ain't g-g-g-g-got no money, but he probly owes me nine hh-h-h-h-hunnert dollars, more or less."

I thought some more. "Harce, don't you have a hog you can sell to help Ponytail out? He needs to pay off the entire loan or he will be paying interest for the rest of his life and the truck will wear out and he won't have anything."

This startled Harce. "Queenie? You want me to sell Queenie? She'd bring enough money, but I love Queenie. I don't think I could bear to part with her. Queenie is the only friend I got now that Louann is done gone. I go out and talk with her every night. She don't never say anything bad to me and she loves me. Do you know what they would do with Queenie if I sold her?"

"Make bacon?"

"Yeah, make bacon and make fatback and make chitlins. I cain't think about it."

"Well, you better think about it."

Harce jumped up, spilling what was left of his coffee on the front of his shirt. "I'll tell you what I'll do. I'll just get me a job." He stopped and thought for a moment. "Hey, John, you know where I can get a job?"

I grinned. This was what was needed for the situation. "I think Mullinax needs a back hoe operator." I said. "I'll call him and tell him how good you are with a back hoe and a dozer. I think he's working on a road on Lavender Mountain. He'll probably pay you ten dollars an hour."

"Who's Mullinax?"

"He's this guy I know who used to build roads for the coal mines up in West Virginia. He's about as crazy as you are, Harce. He moved down here on account of his wife and he takes on the jobs that no one else wants."

Harce liked that one. "Well, call him, John. I can make a back hoe sit up and talk. Maybe that will keep me from being so lonesome. I'll try it out. Maybe with that and cutting wood I ain't got to sell Queenie."

So I promised to call Mullinax. The coffee was gone and I was ready for a nap.

I grinned at Harce. "I think it's time for you and Ponytail to go home so I can rest."

They headed for Ponytail's truck. Harce grabbed the door handle and turned. "Hey, John, I need to borry forty dollars."

I froze.

Forty dollars is the magic number that people need to get a bag of some kind of drugs. I had no idea what kind they got, I just knew that this was the price for a bag of marijuana or for many other things. Anytime someone needed to feed a habit, it always cost forty dollars. I reached in my pocket. "Here, Harce. Here's five dollars for a six-pack. That will get you by."

He took the five dollar bill and left.

chapter 29
CELL PHONES IN THE COLONS

In the fall of 2002, the cell phone was changing the social structure of the world. I had decided that I really didn't need a cell phone and I was in the minority. I still enjoyed using the old phone on the wall in the kitchen. When the rednecks asked me why I didn't get one, I told them, "I once talked with a wise old man who said, 'It's a pore man that has a bell in his house that anyone in the world can ring.'" Then, I would smile and say, "It's a really pore man who has a bell on his belt that anyone in the world can ring." Everybody seemed to think that statement funny.

Most of the rednecks had had trouble with Southern Bell and therefore had no telephone at all. A lot more of them had credit problems which meant that they had to pay Cingular or Verizon a large deposit to get one.

Very few of the rednecks from The Colons had a checking account. They would deal in cash. The Friday afternoon lines were long at the banks and at the check-cashing desk at Randolph's Warehouse Beverage Center, where one could get a payroll check cashed for a two dollar charge plus a five per cent surcharge.

I watched one day as George Johnson made a complicated transaction at Randolph's. He took his check from the Mohawk carpet mill up to the desk. Randolph punched the amount of the check into his modified cash register which subtracted the two dollar fee and then subtracted the five per cent. Randolph counted out the cash. George Johnson counted the money and complained about the charge. Randolph told George that he wasn't making a profit on the transaction on account of insurance. I figured that Randolph was just providing the check-cashing service out of the goodness of his heart.

George then pulled out a list of important bills that needed paying. He got a money order for the television cable, another for the rent/purchase payment on his couch and big screen television, and yet another for his house rent. Each money order cost an extra fee. George would handle everything else in cash. George's first cash transaction was usually a case of Budweiser. He would then take the money orders and deliver them to the proper payment locations.

I had asked Bud about this method of doing business and he told me how it worked. "Well, see, Grandpa and Daddy did business the same way, sort of. 'Course, they didn't have to get money orders, but they liked to sell their cotton, get a check, and then cash it with the same man who done give them the check. Then they would go all over town and buy whatever stuff they needed. It made them feel important to pull out a wad of money and slowly count out the payment. Now, instead of just at cotton pickin time, everybody gets to have money one day a week. They'll always be broke on Monday, but they will have money to spend on Friday night and a little left for Saturday. That's how it works. The man at the cotton block always got his percent. Now, Randolph gets the per cent. It's the same thing, just different times and people."

The large cell phone companies didn't seem to have any understanding of how the redneck economy worked, and when someone didn't have a checking account, a deposit of five hundred dollars or more was required. This put cell phones out of reach for almost all of my redneck acquaintances. They all wanted a cell phone to hang on their belt but they couldn't seem to figure out how to get one. Then someone got really smart and figured out how to market telephone services to anyone who wanted them.

Bud showed up one day. "Look here what I got me." He grinned and handed me a refurbished cell phone. I looked at it, turned it over in my hands, examined the pictures on some of the buttons and handed it back.

"How'd you get that?" I asked. "You told me when you went to Cingular they wanted a five hundred dollar deposit."

Bud grinned again. "There's this here man over on North Broad – you know, where the junk store is – he gets these cell phones and they only cost fifty bucks and then you can buy minutes for them. Come on and go with me. I got to buy me some minutes. I'll show you."

I have always admired good marketing, so I went with Bud down to North Broad to a small store which was full of dust-covered used computers, second-hand stereos and televisions, pictures of Jesus or Elvis painted in bright colors on black velvet, and various and sundry related items. In the back corner stood a very clean, obviously new counter with a sign that read "CELL PHONES." Bud got in line behind a skinny girl with cut-off jeans and dirty blonde hair. A short grey-haired man in a dirty white shirt worked slowly helping another customer. I looked at all of the items on the shelves and admired the paintings until Bud got up to the counter. He yelled at me, "Hey, John, c'mere and watch this. This here's Mister Bornstein, he done figured this here cell phone stuff out."

Bud leaned on the counter, counted out twenty-five dollars in cash, and said, "Gimme twenty-five dollars worth." He handed his phone to Mr. Bornstein who took the money and the phone. He turned his back on the counter, punched a few buttons on a computer terminal and waited until a voice came over the computer saying, "Your transaction has been completed." He handed the phone back to Bud and said, "That gives you a hundred and ninety minutes. Thanks, Bud."

I did a few calculations in my head and thought, "Now, this is better than a pawn shop." I looked behind me and saw that the line had grown and that there were more cars driving up into the parking lot. As we were leaving, I heard someone say to Mr. Bornstein, "How many minutes kin I get for this car stereo?"

Mr. Bornstein replied, "I'll give you a hundred and ninety minutes for it." I had to admire the enterprise, but it was definitely time for me to leave.

Bud and I got in his truck. He started dialing a number on the cell phone. "I'm calling Kickstand. He done got one, too. Any time I call someone it tells me how many minutes I got." He finished dialing and pushed the "call" button. He let me listen to the voice on the phone say, "Thank you for using pre-pay phone services. You have one hundred and eighty-nine minutes of calling time." Then he put the phone to his ear as it started ringing. I heard Bud's end of the following conversation.

"Where you at?"

Pause.

"What you doin'?"

Pause.

"Well, all right, then, I'll see you in a little bit."

When we were almost to the turn-off to my house, Bud's phone rang. He smiled and punched a button. "I'm on my way to take John home. We done went and got some minutes."

Pause.

"I done told you I'm taking John home."

Pause.

"Well, all right, then, I'll see you in a little bit."

He pushed the 'end' button.

"See there, John?" he said. "Now, we kin talk to anybody, any time, any where. You just got to get minutes every now and then."

"Who was that calling just a minute ago?" I asked.

"That was Harce. He done said they was trying to get his welding truck and he was going to your house to hide it in the woods."

chapter 30

STRANGE HAPPENINGS

Looking back, I guess I should have been more perceptive about what happened that afternoon with Harce. Little bits of information had been coming my way for some time, but I just hadn't put them all together. I had heard that methamphetamine, or meth, had made its way to our area from the hills in Tennessee – just as Kickstand had predicted some time ago. I had learned that the police had picked up a lot of pot dealers and that marijuana had become hard to get. Betty Sue had told me that Sobrina the pot dealer was manufacturing some strange, foul-smelling substance in her bathroom. I had read about some meth arrests in the paper, but nothing of much consequence.

Kickstand had told me that the talk going around with the boilermakers indicated that meth was prevalent, cheap and available, but to stay away from it because it was highly addictive. He said that when people started meth, they had boundless energy and a high that was much different from smoking pot, but that after a while it "kills your appetite, and the lack of sleep makes you see things, and it makes you think that everybody is after you." I took the last part of that to mean paranoia.

At any rate, drugs were not on my mind as Bud took me home from the cell phone store. I got out of his truck, thanked him for showing me the cell phone, said, "See you in a little bit," and walked in the house for a cup of coffee. As I walked back outside with my coffee, I heard the rattling of Harce's welding truck coming up the driveway. He was coming fast. Harce was driving, alone, and he didn't even wave as he sped up the hill past the greenhouse and parked the truck behind some cedar trees. He got out of the truck, slammed the door, and came down the hill with his gimpy sort of walk. He was moving fast. I went back in to get him a cup of coffee and refresh my own.

"Here's some coffee for you," I said as he walked up to me. "What in the world is going on with your welding truck?"

Harce sipped his coffee. "I was hoping I could leave it here for a while, John. I need to hide it. They're after it."

I looked him in the eye. His eyes seemed sort of confused. He also looked like he had lost weight.

"Who's after it?"

"I don't know. I just need to hide it here for a while. How about you take me home?"

I didn't want to hear that. I had just gotten home and I didn't feel much like driving to The Colons.

"Tell you what, Harce. I'll take you home after I sit on the dock a while and drink my coffee. You need to tell me what's going on with your truck."

"I don't know. I just know they're after it and I need to hide it here for a while."

"Well, then, tell me about your job with Mullinax. How's that going?"

"I appreciate you getting me the job, John. He hired Ponytail to he'p him, too and we done him a bunch of work and I taken the money an me and Ponytail paid off his truck at the title pawn shop. I'm glad you told me to do that. Mullinax done told me that me and Ponytail worked harder and faster than anybody ever did and that was the problem. We done finished the job too soon and he had to lay us off til he got another one."

"So, what are you doing now?"

"Well, I run some wood through the sawmill that done had some nails in it and it messed up the blade and so me and Ponytail is cutting firewood to sell so I kin get a new blade for it. I had me a couple of girlfriends for a little while but they ain't nothing like Louann, and they ain't stayed around. And I get up there at the house and I get lonesome and I don't sometimes know how to live with it. And now they're after my welding truck."

"Who's after your truck?" I asked again.

"I don't know who it is. I just know they're after it." He had the confused look again.

We finished our coffee, got in the truck, and headed toward Harce's house. I didn't get a word in edgewise during the entire trip. Harce talked nonstop about building the road with Mullinax, short time girlfriends he had run across, and being lonely. He spent a lot of time telling me about being lonely. He said he had tried to find Louann but that she was "hidin' out somewhere." My ears were tired when I finally pulled into his driveway. He got out and turned to me. "Hey, John, come over here and look at the gazebo. There's something I didn't tell you." I was ready to go, but the way he looked roused my curiosity. I got out of the truck and walked over to the gazebo. He pointed at the roof. I looked up at the carefully split and installed cedar shingles. I was startled to see sunlight shining through several holes.

"Harce," I said. "What in the world happened to the roof?"

"It was weird, John. I come out here the other night about three o'clock in the morning and I looked and I jumped back on the porch and I looked again and there was this whole bunch of po-lice out there in the yard."

My eyes opened wide. "Police? How many? What were they doing?"

Harce pointed to the fence line. "They was a bunch of them over there looking up and down the fence line and they was some more looking all inside the smoke house and I done went and crawled into the gazebo and looked and they was four of them cops up on the roof crawling around."

I had the picture in my head, but I couldn't believe it. "What were they looking for?" I asked.

"I don't know what they was looking for but I guess they must of thought I had some dope or something 'cause they was running all over the place."

I was having trouble processing this information. "What did you do?"

"I didn't know what to do so I crawled in the house and got my 30-30 and I come back outside and I started shooting at them sumbitches. I hit a couple of them, too. Then I run over inside the gazebo and I done started shooting up into the roof. I couldn't see them sumbitches up there but I knew they was up there and I figured I could get some of them. I started shooting and they started falling off the sides and then I figured they was gone and I went to sleep on the gazebo floor with my rifle in my hand."

My mind was reeling. "What happened when you woke up the next morning?"

He shook his head. "That's what's so strange, John. I knowed I hit a bunch of them and the 30-30 packs a punch. I looked all over the place and there warn't no dead cops and I looked for blood and there warn't no blood. The only thing I saw was them two fence posts blowed all to hell and back over there and a whole bunch of holes in the top of the gazebo." He gave me a quizzical look. "I don't know where they all went or why they ain't been back here to arrest me."

It was definitely time for me to leave. I opened the truck door and turned to Harce. He was just standing there shaking his head.

I asked, "Is that who is after your welding truck?"

"Naw, they're after it."

"Who is they?"

He looked at the ground. "I don't know. I just know they're after it. I cain't let nothing happen to my welding truck."

I think the only time I ever left somewhere so fast was when I was in high school and I heard the principal coming around the corner to catch us smoking. I was out of there. I dodged all of the pot holes in the road and made it home in record time. I got some coffee and sat on the dock with my eyes closed, thinking. I must have gone to sleep, because it was dark when I looked up. I couldn't get the cops on the gazebo out of my head.

I wondered what would happen next and I found out three days later. I was working on getting the leftover begonias ready to put in the greenhouse for the next spring's hanging baskets. Ponytail and Harce drove up to the greenhouse and got out of the truck. Harce moved rapidly around the truck and said, "I come to get my welding truck. Thanks for letting me keep it here."

I looked at him. He was definitely losing weight. I asked, "So, Harce, all of a sudden they aren't after your truck? What happened?"

He was serious. "Well, they had to get someone and when they couldn't find my truck, they decided to burn Sobrina's house down."

"Sobrina's house burned down? When did that happen?" I asked.

"Last night. They must of bombed it. There was this big boom and then lots of far. It was gone when the far department got there. I ain't seen Sobrina, neither. They must of kidnapped her."

I silently reached for my thermos and poured some coffee. Ponytail decided it was time for him to go and he and Harce went over to make sure the welding truck would start up. It did. Satisfied, they turned it off. Ponytail got in his S-10 and started down the driveway and Harce walked over to where I was resting on a stump, drinking my coffee.

"Hey, John, tell me a story. You ain't told me a story in a long time."

Harce was right. I hadn't told him a story in a long time. I tried to think of one, but I was having trouble thinking about anything other than policemen on gazebos and houses burning down. I couldn't tie it all together. Harce came and pulled up a stump next to me. He waited in anticipation as I tried to get a story started.

"Well, there was the time when Bud was a kid and they decided to steal some watermelon . . ."

"I done heard that one."

"How about the three-legged bird dog?"

He grinned. "That's the one that pulled the man out from under the tractor? I done heard that one."

I thought for a while. "How about the one about the prostitute who fell in love with the Mormon preacher who already had eleven wives?"

Harce grinned and shook his head. "I done heard that one, too.

Let me tell you what happened to me the last couple of days."

I wasn't sure that I really wanted to hear what happened to him, but I sat and waited, anyway.

He leaned back and stretched out his legs and arms. Then he sat up, brought in his feet, and rested his forearms on his knees. "You ain't gon' believe this stuff, John, but I made me some new friends the other night."

I interrupted, "New friends? Who are they?"

Harce laughed. "They ain't 'who,' they's 'what.' See, there's these little birds. Sparrows, I think they are. Or maybe they are something else, cause they have these blue and yellow stripes. Anyhow, they are these little birds and they come around to see me and one of them will sit in my hand and when I close my hand around him, I get small, just like he is. What do you think of that?"

I stared at Harce. "Harce, are you for real?"

He laughed. "I knowed you wouldn't believe me. Yeah, these birds are real and I get really small and that ain't all."

He paused and looked out over the trees.

"See, when I get small, then all I have to think about is where I want to go and they will take me there. Like I told one of them birds that I wanted to go see Kickstand and I got small and they took me to see him at his house. And they made him small, too, and me and him drunk a bunch of beers and talked about all kind of stuff. Then the birds flew me back home and the next morning I called Kickstand and told him I had a good time and he didn't remember it. He must of drunk too many beers."

Harce paused. "Hey, John, you got any more coffee in that thermos?"

I got up and poured him some coffee in a styrofoam cup. I sat down, watched him take a sip, and waited for him to resume his story. I had no idea where he was going. I thought maybe there was a punch line coming.

Harce got a beatific look on his face. It reminded me of the time I watched an evangelist calling down Jesus' love on the congregation.

"Well," he continued, "well, then the next night, them birds come and got me and they taken me to see my granny. And she was alive

again, too. I don't know how them birds made that happen. And they
made her small like me, too. I told her about my leg and all, and when
I looked down, my leg was all well and real and like it was before the
motorcycle accident. But, anyhow, I talked to grandma and all for a
long time and me and her laughed about the funny stuff and then we
talked about how sad it was when Granpa died and she done told me
she had seed him the other day. Me and her walked around the yard
and looked at her flowers and then she done told them birds it was
time to take me home. I didn't want to go, but them birds minded her
like they always done."

I looked at him long and hard. "Harce, you are dreaming all of
this. That sort of thing doesn't happen."

He looked me straight in the eye with a high level of
concentration showing on his face. "That's what I thought." He
looked off into the sky. "I thought I was dreaming of something but
it really happened. He took a sip of coffee and continued, "Then
last night I ast them birds to take me to find Louann. They shrunk me
down and me and them went everywhere I ever been with Louann.
I stopped and asked about her and all the people I talked to they was
small like me 'cause the birds made them that way."

He stopped and looked at the ground. "All them people done told
me I didn't treat her right and to leave her alone. Then the birds took
me home."

Harce stretched out his right leg and stuck his hand in his pocket
like he always did when he was preparing to roll a joint. I watched as
he instead pulled out a crumpled up piece of tinfoil and a small ceramic
pipe. I didn't really know what he was doing, but an alarm went off in
my brain when he opened the tinfoil and I saw some yellowish crystals
that looked kind of like little pieces of soapstone.

I jumped up from my seat on the stump, spilling coffee all over
my leg. I shook my finger in his face. "Harce, I don't know what that is,
but it's not going to be around here. Roll up that tinfoil, put it in your
pocket, and get the hell out of here right now."

Harce looked stricken. He knew he had crossed my line. He stood
and stuffed his paraphernalia into his pocket and said, "I'm sorry, John,
it won't happen again. I'm sorry; I'm sorry."

He ran over to his welding truck, cranked it, and stopped as he was passing where I stood. He stopped and rolled down the window.

"I'm sorry, John. I wasn't thinking. I guess I'll go get some minutes for my phone."

And he drove off.

I stood and watched him go.

That was the last time I ever talked with Harce.

chapter 31
THE BLUE HOUSE

I was adjusting sprinkler heads on a sunny fall day when the Mercedes arrived in the driveway. I dried off my hands and stared. The car was quiet, black, and shiny. It was immaculately clean and the windows were heavily tinted. The sun reflecting from the chrome wheels almost blinded me. I never knew much about the model names and numbers for a Mercedes because I never cared, but this was a big, expensive looking four door sedan. I could see the driver through the windshield, patiently waiting with the motor idling. I quit staring at the car and started staring at the man who climbed out of the back door.

He was big. He was obviously Hispanic. He was over six feet tall – maybe about my height or a little under, but he was big. His upper arms filled the sleeves of his white satin shirt. He had wide shoulders and a large muscular chest. I always look for a pot belly on big men but there wasn't one. He must have had about a 36-inch waist with a flat stomach. His upper legs in black slacks were like sculpted tree trunks. I looked at his head on top of a large muscular neck and saw wrinkles that could only be caused by a perpetual scowl. He was clean-shaven. His hair was full and tied back in a short, well kept ponytail. I didn't count the rings on his fingers or the chains on his neck, but there were several. A gold crucifix on a gold chain hung outside his shirt. I wouldn't say that I reacted with fear, but I was startled. This man was as intimidating as any man I had ever seen. I knew who he was. This was the "mean Mexican" who had dealt with Harce.

He tried to smile at me, but even his smile was intimidating. I just raised my eyebrows, stared at him and waited. He spoke first, speaking slightly-accented English in a slightly halting manner which told me he was carefully selecting each word, "Mister Juan?" He grinned an evil grin showing polished white teeth with one gold-rimmed crown. "Mister Juan? My name is Emilio. You will please to come with me." He gestured toward the back door of the car.

"Come with you where?" I asked.

"I am not supposed to tell you. I have been sent to bring you."

"Bring me where? I'm not getting in a car with someone I don't know unless I know where I am going."

"I am sorry, Mister Juan, I cannot tell you where we are going. I have just been sent to bring you. Those are my instructions."

"What if I don't want to go?" I asked. I was becoming very uncomfortable. I was in a fight or flight situation and I didn't think I would stand a chance in a fight. I looked toward the trees behind me. The Mexican giant followed my gaze. His hands were ready at his side. His knees were slightly bent as if in preparation for a cat-like pounce.

"Please don't do that, Mister Juan. I have been told to bring you and to try not to hurt you. I will take you with me as I was instructed. I will try not to hurt you. If I have to hurt you to take you with me, I will do so. If you will just come with me, everything will be all right." I thought about this for a moment and decided that my best chance was to get in the car. Emilio escorted me around to the back door on the driver's side, opened it and gently pushed me down in the seat. He shut the door and I noticed that the inside door handle on my side had been removed. Emilio walked around and got into the back seat on the passenger's side. I tried to relax and sat back into the softest, most body-friendly upholstery I had ever known. I don't think I was really afraid as much as I was curious and apprehensive.

Emilio leaned back in the car and relaxed as it backed out and headed toward the road, taking a right at the end of the driveway and heading out of town on the back roads. He tried his best to be pleasant as he opened a bottle of Perrier for himself. He took a sip, set the bottle in a holder, and reached for a thermos and a cup. "They told me you will like a cup of black coffee." He opened the thermos and poured steaming, black, wonderfully fragrant coffee into a ceramic cup. This made me feel a little better. I had a funny thought about how Bud would come up with a ransom if I was being kidnapped. I grinned at the thought.

Emilio misunderstood the grin and said, "That's better, Mister Juan. Everything will be all right."

I took a swallow of the best coffee I had ever had and made a mental note to find out what it was. Emilio read my mind. "It is hand-picked pure Jamaican Blue Mountain coffee. It is good, is it not?"

I felt like I was riding in a comfortable living room as the Mercedes traveled down the two-lane back roads. I knew the territory and made mental notes of where I was and tried to figure out where I was going. Emilio sat quietly and only broke the silence once to make a request. "Please do not pay attention to where you are going. If someone later asks you where you were, I want you to say you do not know." I just nodded my head and concentrated on the cup of coffee.

We turned left on Highway 140, went over a couple of bridges, and turned right on the four-lane Highway 27 going north. About six miles down the road, the driver made a left turn on Silver Hill Road which ran through wooded hills heading toward the state line.

Emilio pointed out the window and said, "This land reminds me of my home in Mexico, when I was a boy." The driver drove on, never saying a word. We turned right on Highway 100, heading north and then went off on some back roads that I hadn't been on before. I just patiently waited. Emilio was silent, looking out the window with detachment.

Finally, the driver turned into a well-maintained, curving gravel driveway which meandered through a large stand of tall Georgia pines. The gravel driveway circled in front of an older large house with an immense front porch. The columns and trim on the porch were painted a shiny white. The rest of the house was blue. It wasn't light enough to be a sky blue and it wasn't dark enough to be a navy blue. It was a startling cerulean blue.

I was checking everything out when Emilio said, "Please to come with me, Mister Juan." He eased his big body out of the Mercedes and walked around to open the door for me. As I got out, I almost stepped on a chicken that was being chased around the yard by a large rooster. Emilio led me up to the porch and opened the door, motioning me in.

I walked into a large, bright, clean, comfortable looking room with overstuffed furniture neatly arranged against all four walls. Sun streamed in through the south-facing windows, creating splashes and lines of light on the floor. In one of these splashes of light there were three small brown children quietly occupied with coloring books and crayons. A big screen television in one corner produced what seemed to be soap opera dialogue in rapid Spanish. I inhaled deeply, delighted with the fragrant smells of cooking pork, onions, chilis, cilantro and garlic that seeped in from another room. In the back of my mind was the question, "What in the hell am I doing here?"

Emilio placed his hand in the middle of my back as gently as he could. I staggered forward. He spoke. "Come with me, amigo. I will show you why I was sent to bring you." He guided me through a door heading towards the back of the house. I walked into a country kitchen which reminded me of farm kitchens from my youth. I saw two Mexican women working on one side of the kitchen. One of them was cutting up piles of onions, peppers and cilantro while the other was forming balls of corn dough and making tortillas in a hand-operated press. Off to my left I saw someone in the classic Spanish position, sitting on the floor, leaning against the wall, wearing a serape and a large brimmed sombrero, knees up with arms wrapped around them, and the head down with the hat brim covering the face. Whoever it was seemed lost in sleep, meditation, or other silent reverie. Emilio said, "Look around, amigo and see what you see."

I walked over and checked out the cooking. I looked around at the light pink walls with red trim on the windows and doors. Lots of light was streaming through the windows, offering a canvas for a design made of slowly rising tendrils of steam and vapors. My stomach started growling as each of the two cooking women smiled and said, "Ola, señor Juan."

I didn't know any of them. One of the cooks gave me a big smile and nodded toward the figure sitting on the floor in the corner in a manner which suggested there might be something interesting there. I walked in that direction and stood in front of whoever it was. The head slowly raised up so I could see the face.

I knew it was Louann. She looked up at me with the biggest grin I had ever seen on a woman. She was beautiful.

"Hi, John," she said sweetly. "I just had to see you one more time and let you know I was all right." She laughed at the look on my face and smiled widely. The Mona Lisa smile was gone and she displayed beautiful white crowns and caps which were the evidence of the work of a brilliant dentist. Louann jumped up, dropped the serape and sombrero and gave me a big, dancing hug.

"I sent Emilio for you 'cause I didn't want nobody but you to know where I was. I know Harce is been looking for me and I still care about him, but if he caused any trouble, he would get hurt and I don't want that." She looked at the floor for a moment, thinking. "I'm happy, John. Manuel loves me and I love him and he treats me like a lady. Nobody never wanted to be married to me before, but Manuel does. I like being married." She pirouetted gracefully, arms out to include her surroundings. "And here there is flowers and chickens and . . ." She looked at the floor again and slowly looked me in the eye. "And children. There's children for me to play with and to feed the animals with and to smell flowers with. I like that."

I looked around and asked, "Where's Manuel? Is he around?"

She said, "Naw, he ain't here. His grandpa just died and Manuel's gone to Mexico to see about the funeral. He loved his grandpa. In Mexican, they call it 'abuelo.' That's Mexican for grandpa. His grandpa had this nice ranch in Mexico and I didn't have no papers so I cain't go with him, but he will be back in a few days. I sure do miss him. He's good to me."

Louann and I talked for a while about things that weren't important. We walked outside and looked at the chickens and the flowers and the children playing in the back yard. She looked good and she seemed very happy. Seeing her big, beautiful, open grin brought

tears to my eyes. I always get tears in my eyes about stupid things like
that. I watched as she chased a wayward ball and threw it back to the
children. She was laughing and yelling, "You kids got to learn how to
catch that thing if you ever going to play pro baseball." Louann looked
as if she was gaining a lot of weight. I started to say something about
it when Emilio walked up. He said, "Mister Juan, we got to take you
home, now. Please to come with me."

Louann followed me out to the Mercedes. She touched me on
the arm and said, "It's good to see you, John. In about a week, you kin
tell Kickstand and Ponytail that I said goodbye. Manuel's grandpa
has done left him the ranch in Mexico and we're going to go live
there. Now that I am Manuel's legal wife I can be a Mexican citizen.
Manuel wants me to teach them people down there how to make
Brunswick stew."

I got in the Mercedes, looked out the open door and said, "Louann,
I wish you the best of everything. See if you can write me a letter some
time." One of the cooking ladies ran out from the house and handed
me a heavy bag that smelled heavenly. I knew I wouldn't have to worry
about dinner that night. I smiled and said, "Gracias."

She smiled at the ground and replied, "de nada."

I waved at Louann and closed the car door as the driver put the
car in gear and drove off.

Louann stood there waving until we drove out of sight. I could
have sworn she was pregnant.

chapter 32
THE PHONE CALL

I was asleep when the phone rang. Marsha had been in the other room watching television. I remember looking at the clock and wondering who in the hell was calling my house at eleven-thirty at night. I could hear Marsha's voice through the open bedroom door. "Hello?"

Pause.

"Yeah, ok, I'll tell him."

Then there was a noise as she slammed the receiver down on the phone cradle. I heard stomping approaching the bedroom.

"You awake?"

"Yeah, now I am."

"Harce wants you to get him out of jail."

I thought about it.

"What's he in there for?"

"He didn't say."

"Well, I'm not going out tonight. I'm tired. It will do him good to stay there for a while. Maybe some time in jail will help him get some of that stuff out of his system."

Marsha turned and went back into the other room. I went back to sleep. I slept well because I had worked hard the day before and I deserved and needed it. I woke up at six-thirty the next morning to the sound of a vehicle pulling into the parking area outside the house. It sounded like Ponytail's truck. I walked outside and discovered that indeed, it was Ponytail's truck. I watched wearily as he walked up to the porch where I was standing.

"H-hh-hey, John. Harce c-c-c-c-called me last night at about t-t-t-t-ten o'clock on this here cell phone and h-h-h-h-he wants me to tell you to g-g-g-g-g-get him out of j-j-j-j-jail."

"What did he get arrested for?" I asked.

"He t-t-t-t-told me 'eluding.' B-b-b-b-but I don't know w-w-what that means."

"I'll think about it, Ponytail. I think maybe he needs to stay there a while and get whatever is in his body out of his body. What do you think?"

Ponytail studied the situation. "M-maybe you're right, John. He's b-b-b-b-been acting right funny here l-l-lately, and he's b-b-b-b-been very sad and l-l-lonesome."

Ponytail left. I went in to brew my morning coffee and ponder the situation.

After I had drunk a couple of cups of coffee, lost in thought, I decided to call the jail and find out the circumstances of Harce's arrest. I dialed the phone.

"County jail."

"Hey, I wanted to find out what Harce is charged with."

"Harce?"

"Yeah, you know Harce, don't you?"

"Of course, everybody here knows Harce. I just don't remember seeing his name on the list. Let me check."

There was a long pause with computer keys clicking in the background.

"Harce ain't here."

"Well, he called me from jail."

"Well, he didn't call you from this jail."

I hung up the phone. I was confused and mystified. Then I reasoned, maybe it was the Bartow County jail he called from. After all, I thought, The Colons border the next county. I called them. No Harce.

Now, I was really confused. I called the jails in all of the surrounding counties. I called the police department. No one knew anything at all about Harce. The nice lady at the police department said she would try to find out where he was in jail. I gave up and went to work.

chapter 33
HARCE 2003 REVISITED

When they found his leg in the poison ivy patch they knew they were close. One of the cops hollered out, "Hey, John, what does Harce's leg look like?"

I started in his direction, answering, "Blue titanium with a rounded plate on the bottom. Kind of like it was made out of the shank from an expensive tennis racket."

"Well come over here and look."

I looked at the undergrowth in the clearing where the cop was standing.

"No, you come over here!" I yelled. "Didn't your daddy teach you about poison ivy?"

The cop jumped back and ran out to where I stood. He must have been a Yankee.

He was holding the leg. It looked like Harce's leg, but there was one way to make sure.

I pointed to it. "Turn it over and look just above where the ankle would be. There should be a small, almost invisible sliding plate. That's where he kept his pot."

A detective walked up and examined the leg. He found the plate and slid it to the side, obviously admiring the craftsmanship. The hole was empty.

Bud had called me that morning and told me that the police needed help finding Harce. They had found his truck stuck in a ditch and figured he was lost in the woods behind the bauxite quarries. Bud and I knew he wasn't lost. We knew something bad was wrong. Harce would never get lost in those woods.

Bud explained it to the detective. "Officer, there ain't no way Harce got lost in them woods. He was a carpenter—"

"Bud, what does that have to do with it?"

"I'm getting there, officer. You see, Harce could build anything you want. Do a real good job, too. But he never understood fences."

"Bud, I don't see how that enters into—"

Bud bowed up. His face turned red, and he got that look on his face that told the detective to shut up.

"Jest give me a minute and I'll tell you. You see, Harce couldn't never build a fence that was worth a damn and his cows and hogs and chickens kept getting out. Before his leg got cut off, he chased every animal he ever had all over every square inch of this mountain. He knew these woods. He knew them like the back of his hand. He knew these woods so well that you sumbitches never even found his dope patch or his still. He ain't lost."

They found Harce's body about an hour later. He had crawled up under some brush that had fallen across a ditch. They pried his cell phone from his stiff fingers. The detective checked to see who Harce had called last.

I looked at the number. I looked at the detective. "That's my number," I said. "He called my house the night before last." I knew right then what had happened.

Bud looked at me and said, "Aw, hell, John. Does that mean....?

An article in the local newspaper the next day read, "He died from a chemical imbalance."

I thought that was a nice thing for them to say.

After the funeral, Kickstand gave Bud and me his thoughts on what happened.

EPILOGUE

"I tried to help him."

Kickstand sat with his elbows on his knees, his hands propping up his head as he looked down at the dock, staring at nothing. He shook his head.

"I tried to take him to talk to some people and every time I tried, he took off running in the woods telling me to leave him alone. And he was just too big and too mean and too hyped up for me to force anything on him." Kickstand sat and stared. Ponytail sat on the corner of the dock watching a fishing bobber that went up and down because there was a fish on the hook. He made no effort to reel in the fish.

Kickstand continued, "When Louann left, Harce tried to clean up everything after the party. But he was lonesome. He hadn't lived by his self in a long time. He was sad and he kept telling me what he should of done and what he wisht he had of done. He smoked up every bit of pot that he could get his hands on. That kind of mellowed him out but then he started drinking beer and smoking pot and that made him mean. It made him so mean that you couldn't stand to be around him."

Kickstand sat in silence. I turned to watch a male cardinal which was sitting in the maple tree guarding the bird feeder while his mate ate breakfast.

"Then they had that big pot bust, you know, when they got all them pounds of pot that was coming in from Texas?" Kickstand paused and shook his head again. "They just weren't no pot to be had nowhere, and that's when Sobrina showed up at the sawmill. She had been making that meth stuff that I done told you about. Well, Harce got some of it from her and smoked it up and all of a sudden he felt good and he had a lot of energy and he started doing stuff again instead of just setting around. There was even a couple of women who came around and that made him feel good, but I knew they was jest there on account of they want him to share the meth with them. When he ran out, they went somewhere else.

"Somewhere in there was when you got him that job with Mullinax and I thought the job would make a difference, but he made good money at the job and he paid his bills and had enough left over for drugs. He got crazier and crazier. Then he got to doing some saw milling and he was working so fast and hard he forgot to run his metal detector over the wood and he messed up his saw blade.

"And he got to where he would cook up all kinds of ways to make money to buy the meth with. And he got skinny and he damn near quit eating. That's what got to me. Harce could-out-eat a hungry hog.

"And then he started seeing things. He got to thinking that everybody was out to get him and he started telling me about these birds that taken him everywhere he wanted to go to and he said that when the birds taken him places he was happy. You see, the meth don't make you hallucinate, but the lack of sleep does. And he kept thinking that the cops was after him, but they warn't. The cops hadn't picked up on the meth yet, they was still after pot. And then, in his head, he thought some other people was after him and I never could figure out who it was. I don't think he could, either. It was all in his head."

I broke my silence. "Why is it that no one told me about all of this?"

Kickstand paused before answering. "Every time I mentioned your name, John, he said something about some kind of contract. I never knew what he was talking about."

It was time for me to shake my head. I knew what the contract was.

Kickstand continued, "Then, Sobrina's meth lab caught on fire and her house burnt down. Harce said that the people that was after him had burnt it down. And then he couldn't get no more meth from Sobrina and he kind of went nuts until he found somewhere else to get it. Then it costed more and more and he did more and more stuff to get money to buy it with. When he couldn't get the meth, he was really crazy. I couldn't hardly be around him when he got crazy."

There was a long pause. I finally asked, "So, Kickstand, what was going on the night he died? Where did the phone calls come from? Why did he say he was in jail?"

Kickstand thought long and hard. "I done thought about that a lot, John. The way I figure it, he was out in his pick-up truck and he thought someone was following him. Them pictures in his head done kicked in and to him they was real. He was in another world. The way I figure it, he got to running from the law in his head and he pulled up into the woods as far as he could and then his truck got stuck. He couldn't get it out and then he started running.

"I figure he run and run and then he taken a break to smoke up some more meth. Then he had this picture in his head and in that picture, the cops caught him and taken him to jail and then they made him take off his leg and show them where he kept his dope in that little pocket he made and then they put him in jail.

"All of that happened in his head, don't you see? And then he remembered his cell phone and he probly smoked every bit more of his meth to keep the cops from getting it and he called Ponytail and he called you to get him out of jail. And since you ain't got no caller ID on your phone, you didn't know where he was calling from."

Kickstand stopped to get his breath. "And then, I think all of the meth finally hit his system and his heart exploded. Sometimes I think he was trying to commit suicide."

Ponytail had been staring silently at his fishing pole throughout the conversation. He looked up. He looked me directly in the eye. "Th-th-th-th-that's it," he said, softly.

afterword: THE LETTER

The envelope looked like it had traveled a million miles. The writing on it was in a careful schoolgirl style with smiley faces inside every possible circle. I opened it carefully and found a hand written note and a picture that looked as if it were made with a disposable camera. I grinned when I figured out who it was from. The letter said:

Dere John,

I just wanted you to know I am all rite.
I am happy working with Manuel on his farm
that he got from his dead granpa.
I done taut everybody to make Brunswick stew.
I got chickens and flars and all kinds of animals.
Here is a picture of me and my baby. I am happy.
Say hay to everybody for me.

Love,
Louann

The picture showed a grinning Louann, holding a grinning, healthy, year-old baby which was resting on her hip. I could see mountains in the background and chickens around her feet. I got tears in my eyes.

John Schulz spent his formative years growing up in the Southeastern United States. He received a BSED degree in English from the University of Georgia. With the exception of a short time teaching, John has held many important positions that range from garbage truck driver to ornamental plant grower to hardware salesman in rural Alabama. He has been a landscape designer and installer for thirty years. John currently refers to himself as a "landscape artist" and writer.

John possesses a good ear for dialect, a good eye for local color, an ability to remember countless details of his experiences, and a complex sense of humor and sensitivity. He has paid attention to southern working men and appreciates their varied and unique lifestyles. *Requiem for a Redneck* is a fictional novel created from a mixed compilation of stories, experiences, and observations that John has held on to for many years. He feels that the Redneck culture presents us with a multitude of interesting stories that can only be seen from the inside.

JOHN'S OBSERVATIONS ON THE SOUTHERN REDNECK:

"Rednecks are more than a series of jokes. They are more than a lifestyle, they are a genre. The true redneck knows how to do things. He knows how to work, and he holds a sense of values from generations past.

"I have always admired people who have the ability to get by when faced with demanding circumstances. Hank Williams, Jr. wrote a song a while back titled A Country Boy Can Survive. I agree with that, however, there's a bigger world outside of the redneck culture, and when the average redneck discovers this, it's usually through some quirk of the rules. I am trying to present the redneck as a multi-level survivalist who creatively handles these situations as they are handed to him. That's what makes my story."